Bob

Finding the Family of Killers

Finding the Family of Killers

Bobbie Kaald

Finding the Family
of Killers
By
Bobbie Kaald

Finding the Family of Killers

Copyright @ 2021 by Bobbie Kaald

KDP ISBN number: 9798592439186

All rights reserved. No part of this book to be re-produced or transmitted in any form or by any means: electronic, mechanical, including photocopying, recording, or by any information storage and retrieval system; without permission in writing from the copyright owner.

This is a work of fiction. Names, characters, places, and incidents either are the product of the author's imagination or are used fictitiously, and any resemblance to any actual person, living or dead, events or locals is entirely coincidental.

Bobbie Kaald

Dedication

In this year of 2020, with Covid-19 and Forest Fires, I have lost many friends. Today, I lost another wonderful woman from my life. She fought cancer two times around and has been released to share with the angels in heaven.

I dedicate this book to Nora, who died on the forty-seventh anniversary of finding a new way of living. She shared a little of that with me and a lot with many others. I miss her more than I can say.

Finding the Family of Killers

Bobbie Kaald

Preface

Life went on after the death of Bill. Michael returned to college with weekly meetings at the DA's office. He told the DA that he was nervous around the girls, but they all seemed to have boyfriends, and it wasn't really an issue. This was the truth as far as he knew.

Wolfe returned to working at the grocery store and seemed to be blending back into his old life. He admitted to the DA during his weekly meetings that he found himself looking over his shoulder for the other men to return.

Agent Roberts completed his retirement from the FBI and began a new type of life as a homeowner. Yardwork was new to him and his weeds were larger and more numerous than the neighbors.

Officer Johnson and Soffia went on a well-earned, month long vacation driving around the continental states. It was a harrowing experience and Soffia was grateful to arrive home in one piece. "Natasha, I am so extremely glad you were here watching the house for us. At least, I didn't have to worry about that. After we saw an RV drive off a cliff on Sonora Pass, I just wanted to come home."

Finding the Family of Killers

"I am glad that it wasn't you. Did anyone die in the crash?" Natasha was packing to go home but turned around to look her mother in the eye for the response.

"A husband and wife died in the crash. We stayed until the rescuers arrived and then drove the rest of the way across the pass with judiciously slow speed." Soffia spoke as if it was normal but tears began to run down her face and her hands began to shake more than a little.

"Mom, were you scared? Are you doing okay now?" Natasha moved closer to her mother and began to put her arm around, but just then her mother stood up straight.

"I was a little scared but very glad that James was able to stop before we went over right behind them." Soffia answered in her brave voice but stopped talking because she suddenly shivered. Then, she changed the subject. "How is Helena? Is she still working for you?"

"She is." Natasha answered.

A couple of months later:

Bobbie Kaald

Table of Content

It Resumes 13
College 18
Holed Up 21
Fear 25
Memories 29
Alone 34
The Discovery 39
Vacation 41
Helena 44
Cemetery but Not 49
The Hunt 53
A New Player 56
Bitter Reunion 59
Missed Again 63
Family Reunion 68
Grand Coulee 73
Soffia 77
Tory 82
Junkyard 87
Missing 92

Finding the Family of Killers

Disaster 96
It Begins 101
The Chase 108
The Bakery 115
Phillip 120
Reunion 123
Natasha and Helena 130
The Search 132
The Bakery 136
Open 139
Growing Family 144
Murder Board 146
The End? 149
The Chase 153
Bones Surface 157
A Spark 160
James 165
Help 168
Zeke's yard 172
Roberts arrives 178
Phillip 183
The Morgue 186

Bobbie Kaald

West Coast Central	190
Volcanic Ash	193
Another Field	197
Tory and Phillip	204
Vincent Arrives	206
Breakfast Reveal	211
Identifying	214
Morning	220
Transportation	223
Tory	227
Vincent	232
Tory	235
The Dump Sites	240
Sargent Salmi	243
Phillip	247
The Call	250
The Capture	254
The Boy	258
The Article	265
Cold Case Again	268

Finding the Family of Killers

Bobbie Kaald

It Resumes

A few months passed, and Isaac was feeling nostalgic for his bakery. He missed his life there a great deal and didn't think anyone would be looking for him. Dig though he might, he was unable to find his former identification papers. He decided to throw caution to the wind and Issac resumed his life with the same papers and name, in a small town located in northeastern Washington. This was easy for him because as it turns out it was a volcano eruption that had chased the group of them out of Western Washington. Everyone was wearing face coverings of any kind to keep the dirt out of their mouths. The goggles he wore were an added touch which kept people who were in the

Finding the Family of Killers

know from recognizing him even if there was a flier out on him. He had not seen one, but he never went in the police station. The post office didn't have a wall of shame with fliers or even missing person's fliers.

There were many people like Isaac in Eastern Washington. Displaced by the quantity of ash and debris that filled the sky from the explosion of the volcano. It rained down on them for too long to remember and Isaac basically just told the truth of his escapade if anyone asked him. He just did not name names.

Isaac could not return home right away because the roads into his town were closed to citizens for a long time after the mountain blew shards of itself high into the sky. Isaac bought a small storefront with an apartment over it here in small town Eastern Washington. It contained sparse furnishing for both the store and the apartment and Isaac planned to spend his time cleaning it up and organizing. Few people spoke to him or interrupted. Most just walked by without looking.

Isaac wanted some fresh bread but for that he needed an oven of any kind. The biggest problem besides not having an oven was the filth that permeated every crevice. He wanted to ask the fire chief to hose the place down, but they were busy with stalled cars, cars on fire, fires of every kind. He didn't know that Agent Roberts used fire hoses to clean out the warehouses he set up to find Isaac and the others.

There weren't any trucks to rent because the air filters were choked with impermeable rock dust from the mountain. He

Bobbie Kaald

guessed they called it ash, but he just thought of it as a lifestyle threatening nuisance. To prepare for moving in, Isaac brought in a bucket and a gallon of Pinesol and a mop. He walked across the dust coated floor leaving telltale footprints everywhere that he stepped. He wore his dust mask at all times and entered the war zone.

Isaac went to the kitchen and put everything on the floor. Lifting the bucket into the sink, he turned the faucet, but no water came out of the faucet. Red rust dripped and a pipe rattling noise nearly deafened him. He turned it off and cursed loudly.

"I am sleeping at an expensive place again tonight!" Isaac exclaimed and then left muttering under his breath all the way to his car. He did stop long enough to shut and lock the front door. Who would ever willingly go inside such a filthy place?

In the morning, Isaac stopped for breakfast at the only breakfast restaurant in town. It was as old as all the towns in Eastern Washington with brown booths whose covers were cracked everywhere. Some of the cracks were covered with duct tape. There was also a counter edged in chrome with multiple cracks along its surface. The top was Formica of an undetermined linage and aged to a beige color or yellow, who could say.

Finding the Family of Killers

While Isaac ate, he asked a few of the regular men who came in for breakfast. "Excuse me, can anyone tell me how to get the water and power on at my shop?"

This brought gales of laughter from everyone. The man at the end of the counter was in the middle of his first drink of coffee and it ended up in droplets down the counter to just in front of Isaac. He coughed and laughed and apologized all at the same time.

"Nice shot." Isaac said in a fake Southern drawl.

When the laughter died away, the man next to Isaac spoke up. "I ran into that same problem myself because no one told me the rules. When the building is empty, they turn the water off. Seemed straight forward to me. That is until I went on a long weekend and returned to a home without running water."

"For the weekend? For the love of …..why?" Isaac cut his thought short because he just met these men, but he needn't have worried.

"That is word for word what I said to them on Monday after spending the night unable to flush my toilet. Of course, I said the word you bit your sentence short on." The man took a drink of his now cold coffee and continued. "They told me it was for my protection just in case the temperature should drop below freezing and the pipes might burst. In August, I ask you, is that even a possibility." He laughed again and smiled.

"Not even." Isaac had finished eating and sat back. "That tells me why it is off, but not how to turn it back on." He stood

Bobbie Kaald

up and smiled at the morning shift. "Thanks for the information. I will remember when I leave for a week-end." He turned to go but someone at the counter called after him.

"Isaac, I turned it on late yesterday. The guy who sold you the shop sent me through a notice about the sale. He probably sent one to the power company as well. Have a good day." When Isaac turned to look, everyone at the counter had their backs to him and were just drinking their coffee.

'Nice group of men.' Isaac thought to himself as he left. He walked here and planned to walk to his shop. All the cleaning things were still inside where he left them. Maybe he could get something done today. He paid for his food and walked out to get on with his day.

Finding the Family of Killers

College

Michael returned to school as per his parole rules. He didn't feel the same there and asked his parole officer, James, if he could quit school for a while. He had acquired his GED and that would be enough to work with James.

James reluctantly agreed to Michael's request. "I think that a transfer next quarter to Edmonds or another college could help." James answered Michael's question with a suggestion but didn't want Michael to be idle and have a lot of time to think about things. He needn't have worried about idle time.

"Hmmm. Is there any food to eat or do you want me to go buy us something good to eat?" Michael was tempting James on purpose because he knew that James was trying to diet.

Bobbie Kaald

"I already ate. You can go eat. Come back in an hour or so and we can go over a work assignment for you." James tone of voice was deep and filled with disgust. He didn't want to offend Michael but Soffia's cooking was pushing his waistline to the point of discomfort in these slacks the mayor made him wear.

"Really, I'm not hungry just now. I was only wondering." Michael sat down in front of James desk with a crooked smile on his face. "What do we need done?"

James mouth dropped open as he realized that Michael was just playing with him. "You are just mean. You know that I want to lose about ten pounds. Go make certain the files are in order. You know how people put them away every which way. I spend days finding some of them after I let anyone else put them away. At least you know how to correctly alphabetize."

"And what order would you like? Numerical, alphabetical, Dewey decimal?" Michael's eyes were sparkling as he asked this, but he was already getting up and made it out of the office before James could answer.

James watched him go. He was sad inside because Michael was so fun loving even though Bill, Tory, and Sam had abused him for so many years. He wondered who Michael would be today if Michael was not kidnapped by this group of sick men, one of whom killed Michael's mother, maybe in front of him.

Michael smiled all the way to the file cabinets. Most of these files were in the computer now. He wanted to box these up but

Finding the Family of Killers

would wait to suggest this until after he sorted through them and put them in order that James required. This would be easier on his back for the most part.

Around noon, Roberts opened the door. "Anyone ready for lunch?" He glanced around and saw that Michael was head-first into the file cabinets and James was sitting behind his desk. He didn't get an immediate response until he started to leave.

"I could eat." Michael nearly whispered. He was smiling all the time and watching for Roberts to start to leave.

"I wasn't asking you, Michael. James are you going to come to lunch?" Roberts yelled into the air.

"Yeah, I'm coming. Michael, you might as well come, too. I will get more work out of you if I feed you." James laughed at Michael and winked at Roberts.

Life was good for the three friends. James didn't think of himself as Michael's parole officer, and Agent Roberts was now officially retired, and Michael was Roberts housemate.

Bill was dead and the other two vanished into the night. None of the weekly faxes that James sent out ever returned a sighting. The two were seemingly like Sasquatch. James knew they existed, but he had no proof of existence. No one ever saw one and lived to talk about it.

Bobbie Kaald

Holed Up

Tory took Bill's advice and resurrected his former self for about an hour. It was then that he remembered all the felony warrants that he never checked on. He was a wanted man in six states. As he sat in his dilapidated old house back in the woods, Tory pulled out his papers from the crimes and found only the ones for theft and property damage that was new enough to be prosecuted.

The statute of limitations had long since run out on all of them. The only thing making any of them a felony was the dollar amount associated with the crime. Tory had no charges for kidnappings and no murders. Now that he was older, he stuck

Finding the Family of Killers

to the rules and Tory had not been arrested for anything since he became Tory.

Tory decided to sleep on this decision. When he woke up the next day, he decided not to risk some police officer in a small town remembering his former name. So, like Isaac, Tory remained Tory. He had gone against Bill's rules before and nothing happened. He didn't know that Bill was dead.

That was a month ago, and Tory went shopping and ate out every day without being discovered. Tory began to feel more confident in his enjoyment of continued secrecy and his feelings of invincibility returned like an armor shell. Now that his car of the moment was up and running again, after spending every waking moment on it, Tory took a drive around. Previously, he only walked for the mile or so into town and back again.

When Tory reached town, he made a mandatory stop at the local gas station and pulled up to a pump. There was a sign on the pump, 'out of unleaded'. That was okay, this old of a car needed leaded and he would probably need an additive before he filled up. Turning the car off, Tory got out but was met by an old dried up man who looked like Isaac's relative. "I need an additive before I fill up. Do you have any for this old beater?"

"Yup, I bring it to ya. You pay'n cash?" The old man asked in his slow and unhurried fashion. He stood there looking at Tory as if he had all day.

Bobbie Kaald

"Here's thirty. Whatever the additive costs, give me the rest in premium." Tory answered him and handed over thirty dollars of his savings. His savings were dwindling. Vagrants carried a lot of cash with them and had been a constant source of income in the past. He might have to resort to killing again. Change came so hard to him. Tory got back into his car and pretended this was a full-service gas station.

It took another thirty minutes for the man to bring out the additive and put the additive in the tank. Then, he topped it off to the penny for the rest of the thirty dollars. Tory took this fairly well. He wasn't in a rush to go anywhere. He watched the man work on his car in his mirrors. Eventually, the man saluted him and began his slow walk back to his front door.

Tory shook his head and started to roll up the window but stopped. He muttered a string of profanities as he started the car and drove out of the station. He left the window down now because his car was full of gas fumes. He never would have let that happen before. Getting old is not for the faint of heart, at least he remembered Bill saying this.

A few miles down the road, Tory rolled up his window and began to relax. He was dressed in his usual manner with a cotton long sleeved shirt and jeans. The only difference is he bought a worn cowboy hat that was a little too large for him. He pulled it down to his ears and eyebrows to disguise himself.

Finding the Family of Killers

Never before had Tory used a disguise, but someone might recognize him from the sketch or even have a picture of him.

Tory was only planning on a short trip. It was almost noon and he would have to turn around in a couple of hours or find a new place to sleep. None of this mattered to Tory. He was out for a relaxation drive, smiling, he went on his way to find whatever he could find. If he found nothing, so be it, he would return to his newest hiding hole or find a new one. This was his way and had always been so for as long as he could remember.

Bobbie Kaald

Fear

Wolfe now thought of himself as Wolfe. It was really his last name, but Michael and the others called him Wolfe. Since his return, he reported to the DA's office once a week and remained on probation for three months. They finally agreed to allow the probation to be expunged from his record. This made his parents extremely happy and Wolfe thought this would fix everything. He was looking forward to returning to his prior life.

As it is with all things, nothing is as easy as wishing for it. This did not fix things. Wolfe returned to work at the grocery where he worked before this all happened. He worked for a week after the probation period, but his co-workers continued to avoid him

Finding the Family of Killers

and look at him as if he were a vampire. He went to his boss and turned in his notice.

Wolfe's boss looked at him when he said he was turning in his notice and answered him. "I am sorry Wolfe. None of this is your fault but no one here is making life easy for you now that you're back. I wish you would try to stay, but I understand if you need to leave."

"I will work out my notice, but after that I must leave." Wolfe was looking at his feet as he said this and just wished for this to be over. He wasn't good with authority figures.

"I am certain that you will be alright, but we are having a slump this month and you will not be required to work the two weeks. I can send the check to your parent's home if that is alright. This way you will have time to find a new job. I will give you a great recommendation, of course." His boss finished speaking and then looked down at his desk as if returning to the prior work he was in the middle of when Wolfe knocked on his door.

This brought a smile to Wolfe, but when he looked up, he kept it off his face, somehow. "That will be okay. I am staying with my folks right now, but I have a lead on a job that will be out of town." Wolfe said his peace and left. After he closed the door, Wolfe whistled the entire way to his truck. He continued to whistle as he entered his parent's home.

Bobbie Kaald

"I'm home, and I quit my job. Everyone acts like I am a killer." Wolfe yelled out as he walked through the house and locked himself into his bedroom.

As it turned out, his parents weren't home. Eventually, Wolfe came out to let them know that he was going out to get some food. No one else was home. He wrote a note and left it on his father's desk before leaving.

Wolfe's dad bought him a Ford pick-up when he got back, but Wolfe wanted a Chev. In a day or two, he might trade it in on a Chev, if he got this new job he was working on.

Wolfe drove through town and right in front of the police station, his truck stopped. "Not here, not now." Wolfe yelled out loud to no one. He didn't want to run into Michael or James or Roberts. He was frozen with terror and could not even turn the key to see if it would start again.

As if that was not bad enough, someone knocked on the window. Wolfe jumped and turned to see Michael staring at him. "No." Wolfe yelled and turned the key. Mercifully, the truck started as if it just took a nap. He drove away at an ever-accelerating speed, forgetting to check if Michael was out of the way.

Wolfe eventually had to slow down and come to a stop or run the red light. His heart was beating at an insane rate and he had broken out in a copious sweat that dripped into his eyes. He

Finding the Family of Killers

could not live in the same town as Michael. This thought just jumped into his mind and took his will from him.

   Wiping his eyes, Wolfe smiled and drove out of town when the light turned green. 'Greener pastures, that's what I need.' Wolfe thought to himself. He needed a vacation and he knew just where to go. Camping was over for the year, and Nachees was calling his name. Forgetting that he learned it with Michael, Wolfe kept a full supply of camping gear in the back of his truck in his new storage unit. He just drove out of town and headed for the pass.

Bobbie Kaald

Memories

Tory wasn't paying much attention to where he was driving. When he came to a turn, he just turned north or east. That way he could get back to his hole without too much trouble. It wouldn't be a problem today because he had already driven too far to return. He would find a new place to stay at least for tonight.

It had been a nice day when he left but the wind was picking up and clouds were coming in. If it rained, he would be sleeping in his car if he didn't find a shelter.

An hour or so later, Tory stopped at a small mom and pop restaurant. He hoped it wasn't the same one from his last time

Finding the Family of Killers

through. After he parked on the edge of the lot, Tory got out and walked into the diner. It was the usual left-over fifties color scheme that had never been updated. It had a black and white checkerboard linoleum floor with chrome edged tables and ripped faded red vinyl bench seats with black tape on them. It was a change from the aged brown vinyl. He almost walked out but he at least needed some coffee.

Avoiding the ripped benches, Tory opted for the counter. He pretended they were clean because he couldn't see anything on the counter, but he avoided looking at the rags they wiped the counter down with. When a waitress walked by, Tory put up a hand and said, "Coffee, please." That usually got him some help.

As Tory mentally predicted to himself, the waitress put her hand out, snagged the coffee pot and grabbed a cup and saucer. About thirty seconds later, she stood in front of Tory pouring him his coffee and it was steaming hot. "Cream and sugar are right in front of you. Can I get you anything else?" She smiled and put her hand on her hip.

"Grilled cheese sandwich?" Tory asked without looking at the menu.

"I think we can do that. Be just a minute." And she was gone.

Tory watched her leave. She stopped briefly to write up his order and tore it off her pad. Slipping it into the wheel, the waitress was off to help the other new customers. Tory liked her efficiency, but he kept his head down using his coffee as

Bobbie Kaald

cover. He would eat quickly but while he waited, he laid a ten-dollar bill on the counter in case he needed to leave before finishing.

On the road again after finishing his meal, Tory felt his confidence returning. Bill had managed to intimidate him again, but Bill was not here leaving his belittling a meaningless mesh of nothingness. Tory read an article from the Herald while he ate about an older man who drove off the edge at Stevens Pass. He was identified by a young man named Michael who was working with the authorities ever since he walked into a police station and announce he had been kidnapped years previously.

It was De'ja' Vue for Tory all over again. As he drove, Tory decided that since he was this close to that farm where he got a truck and the empty campsite by the lake, he might as well head there. Smiling and happy for the first time in an extremely long time, Tory took a left and was soon driving past the farm. The farm clearly seemed to be empty and for this he felt sad and responsible for just a second. He wouldn't need a truck this trip anyway.

Tory soon left the pavement and slowed his speed to keep from raising too high of a dust rooster tail. His wheels jumped up and down on the rocky washboard of a road, but it would

Finding the Family of Killers

only be a couple of miles if he had good luck before he could turn off this gravel road.

When the lake came into view, it was still somewhat daylight unlike the last time he was here. He slowed dramatically to stay on the road and look for any people or vehicles. He would have to move on if there were any. He didn't see any by the lake, but the other half was somewhat shaded by trees and shrubs.

An eagle flew over the lake just before it turned and was lost to his view. It was nice to have wildlife coming back after the forest fire.

Tory drove another hundred feet and nearly stopped to make his next left. With his foot on the brake pedal, he coasted down the deeply rutted hill with large rocks protruding from the compact dirt. He scanned around for evidence of campers but saw nothing. Slowly continuing down and then turning to the right because it was more or less straight ahead. Tory drove the car a lap around to verify that he was alone. Stopping across from the outhouse, he turned the car off and got out. It was beautiful here. If it wasn't a campground, Tory might think about moving here.

Tory slowly walked around to savor the solitude and peace. Oh, how he loved the peace. A cool breeze blew against his skin. The lake water was smooth and inviting but he no longer trusted himself to swim. He was afraid that he might drown. He should drown for all the girls he helped do that.

Bobbie Kaald

Tory stood on the edge of the lake until he became aware that the sun was nearly down. The light had faded so slowly that he barely noticed. He turned around and walked over to a bush to relieve himself because there was no light in the out-house, and he didn't have a flashlight. Afterward, Tory went over to his car and rolled down a window a little. Locking himself inside, Tory leaned back and shut his eyes for a few hours of sleep.

Finding the Family of Killers

Alone

Wolfe drove east until the sun went down, but he wasn't tired, and his heart was beating hard and fast inside his chest. He could feel it beating in his neck and inside his head. He needed to calm down. He was aware of how little ability he possessed to accomplish this, but he slowed his car to five miles per hour below the speed limit and took slow deep breaths. This had helped him in the past.

Wolfe rolled his window down a third of the way and felt the cool night air on his face. It blew his hair around a little, but he cut it short after his return with Michael and had been keeping it that way. There were still too many cars to begin using his high beams, but soon he would do that. It was too dark to see

Bobbie Kaald

the countryside that passed him by, but the rockfaces of the hills held no interest to him.

Worrying about deer and elk crossing for a drink, Wolfe slowed down to ten miles per hour under the speed limit. He didn't want to stop, but he might have to take a break.

Finally, Wolfe left the mountains as if he had never been in the mountains. It was always a shock to him when he suddenly entered a town with people and lights and noise. He slowed to twenty-five miles per hour because he missed the speed limit sign, and this was his best guess. Care and caution were always the best course of action while driving, when in doubt.

Wolfe nearly stopped a few times for foot traffic, and again for a car that turned in front of him and then took its own sweet time accelerating to the appropriate speed. Sighing, Wolfe was anxious to reach the other side of town. He kept himself in check because he knew the next few miles would be stop and go as he drove through the small towns bordering this road.

Eventually, Wolfe's car reached the improved highway and he relaxed as his car began to speed down the roadway. It was exhilarating to be free of his family. This is the part of life with Michael that he missed. The difference of course was apparent. He didn't need to feel the fear that always surrounded him when he was with Michael's other 'friends'. He used the term

Finding the Family of Killers

loosely because he knew they weren't Michael's friends, but they weren't enemies, either.

Wolfe became tense again with the memory of his trip of fear. He had avoided Michael the entire time of their probation because of this fear. Fear that Michael would convince him to pal around together. Fear of the other men finding him solely because he was with Michael. Fear of his killing someone just because he was afraid from the trip. Fear of explosive anger. Fear of being a mouse. He was just afraid every minute since Bill asked him to drive him home that day.

Wolfe was in a partial fugue state and when he came to, he was heading north on the far side of the river. It was dark and he was hungry, but he knew that eating would have to wait for morning because everything would be closed to customers this time of night.

The good part about driving in the dark was there were very few other cars on the road coming from either direction. The bad part is living in fear of a deer or elk or even a bear walking out in front of him. He had deer whistles stuck to his front bumper and that seemed to help some, but it did nothing for the fear. His tension settled in his shoulders and neck and he probably would have trouble getting out of the car when he stopped.

Wolfe wanted to pull off for the night, but by the time he saw a pull out on this side of the road, he was past it. So, on he drove. It was helping to get him further away from home and

Bobbie Kaald

Michael, but he was getting tired. He took a deep breath and rolled his window down part way again. He long since turned the heat off. Soon, he would need to turn on the air-conditioner just to stay awake.

Fortunately, Wolfe was quasi awake when he approached the next bridge over the river. He slowed down quickly and made the turn without rolling his vehicle. "Woo, I almost bought it there." He spoke aloud and leaned over as he opened the glove compartment. "Candy, I need that." He spoke aloud now because he wasn't thinking very clearly and seeing a candy bar just tipped the scale.

Wolfe closed the glove box and sat up. He did this quickly and managed to stay on the road, a little swervey but he remained on the pavement. Unwrapping the candy bar quickly, Wolfe jammed it into his mouth and sucked on it.

The sugar went straight into his brain and he felt instantly invigorated. Awakened and more alert, Wolfe drove on. He knew of a few camping areas that were nearly to Canada, but he doubted if he would be able to reach them before he fell asleep at the wheel.

Three towns later, Wolfe drove down into the very first camping area and stopped his truck. Turning the engine off,

Finding the Family of Killers

Wolfe collapsed against the back of the seat, in an instant blissful sleep overcame him.

As Wolfe slept, he slowly slid over to the right and wound up laying on the emergency brake with the seatbelt release eating into his right hip. Even later in the night, he must have felt the pressure of the belt and his hand moved by memory to the buckle release. As he lay down fully, Wolfe sighed and returned to the dream world.

Hours later, the sun came up and eventually flooded his car with light and heat, but Wolfe slept on in his exhausted state. He didn't hear the car driving back down toward town. This is as close as he had come for some time to the men of Michael's world. He did not know how close he came and how fortune shined upon his new freedom.

For Tory's part, he saw the car in the camping ground away from the lake when he drove by. He breathed a sigh of relief that no one discovered his car in the other campground. So close, but so far. Like two predators passing in the night, neither knew of the others presence. Neither wanted to be found. Neither investigated the others presence. Tory smiled as he drove away from the campground into his future without Bill or Sam.

Bobbie Kaald

The Discovery

North of Spokane hiding in a desolate abandoned town lived a man forgotten by the world and aging slowly on his way to leaving it. He needed supplies and to catch up on the news in a creative way that he had used successfully for many years.

Lane walked slowly over to his old Buick given to him by the owner of a junkyard many years ago. It was the only thing left from his life as a murderer, given to him by a murderer. He kept it running with difficulty to remind himself why he still lived here hiding from society. Getting in, Lane tapped the gas pedal twice and turned the key. It started right up but he sat there while the engine slowly smoothed out. He listened for the last sounds

Finding the Family of Killers

of engine clatter to give over to a soft purring sound. This would mean the oil was circulating over all of the metal engine parts.

Lane was getting old but today he had a desire to cruise past his site of disguise and finality. He would be gone a couple of days and then he would be couch ridden for a week while his back recovered from the trip. His hair was long, and his beard seemed longer. It was an optical illusion since his beard started further down his face than his hair. He supposed his hair was white now, but he didn't have a mirror. All of his mirrors where broken by him in a drunken rage when he found his first white hair so awfully long ago that he couldn't remember how old he had been at the time.

Lane didn't have extra gas to burn, so he put the car into drive and began moving toward town. In truth, he could barely see and because of this, Lane drove slowly to allow his slow reactions to have time to catch up to reality.

Reaching town, Lane pulled into the only gas station and the owner came out to fill his tank up with premium. Lane still called it ethyl because that is what the pumps used to say.

"Going on a supply trip, Lane?" The owner asked as he came around to get the fifty dollars that it took to fill up the tank.

Bobbie Kaald

Vacation

The morning after Wolfe left town, Mr. Wolfe, Sr. stopped by the police station to talk to Michael and James. He did not talk to anyone, he yelled out his aggressions and frustrations. Agent Roberts walked in on it and became involved by accident. When he heard the shouting and cursing, Roberts nearly turned around. "Your shouting match can be heard up to the high school. I think we can give them a better example, don't you?"

Mr. Wolfe, Sr. turned and looked at Roberts in the middle of his verbal tirade, but there were no longer any sounds coming out of his open mouth. Putting his arms down, he continued in

Finding the Family of Killers

a markedly lower tone of voice. "I was just explaining that my boy hasn't been home since day before yesterday."

"He was driving out of town toward the mountains the last time I saw him. He very nearly ran me over in his haste to get going. It was still dark, and I guess he really couldn't see me." Michael told James about this yesterday. He knew that Wolfe was avoiding him, and he really didn't blame him a bit.

"Maybe he went to work early to stock shelves?" James asked. He hadn't understood anything that Wolfe, Sr. yelled earlier.

"I told you. He quit his job day before yesterday because they all look at him like he's a killer." Mr. Wolfe, Sr. was starting to get loud again but he saw the look in Roberts eye and stopped talking.

"Well, I take it that no one has seen him since Michael saw him heading east." Roberts looked from one man to another as he spoke. They all nodded their heads. "Well then, I believe Michael and I will try to find some fish or go camping or both. I need a vacation now that I am truly retired."

"Wolfe does keep camping things in his truck ever since I bought it for him when he came back without his car." Wolfe, Sr. remembered that the insurance company reimbursed him for the reportedly stolen car.

"James, is that okay with you?" Michael didn't want to get reported for jumping probation.

Bobbie Kaald

"Yes, it's okay. I need some peace without you asking me for something to do every couple of seconds." James was laughing and thinking that he could go home early tonight.

"I will meet you at home. I need to pack." With that Michael was out the door heading for the house he and Roberts shared. He was running fast and barely looked both ways before running across the main street through town. The very street that Wolfe almost hit him on a couple of days ago.

Roberts waved at the two men who had become his friends and followed Michael out of the office. He shut the door behind himself. He really hoped Wolfe just went to let off some steam somewhere. He was tired of the killer family thing. After all, Wolfe was off parole and currently unemployed. It would be an excellent time for him to take a private vacation trip.

Finding the Family of Killers

Helena

Helena still worked with Natasha at her store. Tonight, she was working until close and would sleep in the store because Natasha was on a vacation of sorts. Natasha went on shopping trips to bring new items into their store. Trips took a while because Natasha was never able to reliably arrive when the managers of the stores that she purchased from were at work. She took numbers and moved on with the thought of circling back. It did not always work out well for Natasha.

Helena opened the front door and pulled down the cage door. It locked automatically when it touched down, and she was the only one with a key besides the fire chief and the police chief. Backing up a little, she swung the door shut and locked

Bobbie Kaald

Natasha's flimsy little lock. Afterward, she placed her New York style bar lock in place and felt a little safer.

Circling back, Helena locked the service door and also installed her new bar lock. Smiling, she grabbed her book from behind the counter and returned to the back room. Pulling the flimsy curtain shut, she sat down at her small table to read and eat her delivery Tai food. Natasha did not like Tai, but she did. She had eaten a lot of Tai while she was on solo duty.

Finished eating, Helena put all of the food containers into a plastic bag and tied it tightly shut. This would help cut down on flies and such. Changing into appropriate sleep attire for away from home, Helena laid down and continued to read until she became tired.

Putting in a small piece of paper, Helena lay the book down next to her in case she couldn't sleep. Pulling up the sheet, she clapped twice, and the back of the store darkened but the front of the store lit up just a little. It was an agreement she had with the police. This way they could see shadows if someone entered the store after closing.

Helena slept easily now. It took about five years for the week of her kidnapping to fade enough to allow her to sleep. She took comfort in Natasha and her family's support during the time since they met. She knew there were still two men unaccounted

Finding the Family of Killers

for but there had never been any sign of them since Bill was found off the edge of the road on the pass, dead.

Morning came and Helena woke up late. Once she came awake enough to look at the clock, she jumped up and hastily dressed. She started to go open up and remembered that her teeth needed brushing. After a quick brush with minty paste, Helena left the back room a pigsty and started opening up. She was late and Natasha was due home today. After opening, she planned to clean up the back room.

When Helena opened the front door to unlock the outer chain cage door, Natasha was just raising it up and they both jumped. "Sleep late, Helena?"

Helena's face flushed with red blotches all over. "Yes, I'm sorry. I need to clean up the back." She turned and walked away to allow her face to return back to her usual pale skin complexion. If she had been born two centuries earlier, she would be the reason the Europeans became known as white.

Natasha turned on the register to let it warm up. "We have a shipment coming in tomorrow. I think you will like it. I found a few new stores who sold me some things just over their own cost."

"That's good." Helena answered in brevity because her mind was on cleaning up the back. "I'm taking out the garbage." The back door shut loudly behind her and opened again with her

Bobbie Kaald

quick return. "Have you called to let your mom know you are back?" They watched each other's back so the parents were never left in the dark.

"No, I haven't, spy. I was just going to call her and let you talk to her with me." Natasha smiled as she spoke even though her voice was sharp. She felt like Helena was the sister that she never had. "I'm calling now. So, get in here." She didn't have to dial because she had a cell phone now and her mom was number two on speed dial. Number one was emergency assistance.

"I'm coming." Helena said as she appeared at Natasha's side.

"Hello? Mom, it's Natasha. I just wanted you to know that I'm home." Natasha spoke softly into the phone because her mother accused her of yelling into the phone and scaring her, once.

"Natasha? Is that you? I'm so glad that you're back. Did you buy a lot of pretty things?" Soffia's voice was soft and distant as if she were only partly listening.

"Mom, yes, it's me. Are you alright? You sound funny." Natasha knew her mother well enough after all these years with everything they had been through to know when she sounded strange.

"Oh, it's probably nothing. Come and see us soon." Soffia was in the middle of hanging up as a way to terminate the conversation.

Finding the Family of Killers

"Mom, if you hang up, I can just call you back." Natasha knew what her mother was about to do and would call her back if she needed to.

"Fine, James told me that Wolfe left town and his father is looking for him, again." Soffia answered and then did hang up. She had things to do and was tired of putting her life on hold ever since her daughter found that grave such a long time ago.

When Natasha heard the click of the phone and then the dial tone, she hung up and then called her mother's number, again. The phone rang about five times and she was nearly ready to hang up herself when her mom finally answered the call.

"I have things to do. Come and visit and we can have a long chat." Soffia pleaded with Natasha.

"Mom, I just wanted to say that I am certain Wolfe has just gone camping. It's the perfect week for it. He probably took time off from his job just for this." Natasha wanted this to be the truth.

"James told me that as well, but he also said that Wolfe quit his job." Soffia answered back and sighed. "I really don't have time to talk right now. Okay? Bye." Then she hung up again, having revealed everything that James asked her not to tell the girls.

Bobbie Kaald

Cemetery but Not

It took longer than Lane remembered to arrive at his destination. He ended up pulling into a wide area for a nap, but he didn't wake up until the next day. He only knew this for certain because the sun was just coming up on the left of the car and the heat of its rays were what woke him up. He woke up sweating from the heat through the glass.

Lane started his car and resumed driving. He wiped his sleeve across his face as he drove. The drive was a monotonous twisty road with trees on both side for the most part and dead grass that never got a chance to do more than sprout. As Lane drove on another thirty minutes, the road finally straightened out for

Finding the Family of Killers

a mile in front of him. He slowed to watch for the expected turn off. He hadn't heard of anyone building out here yet, but this is what he was really looking for. Realtor signs posted would be an unbelievably bad omen.

Lane didn't see any obvious signs of development. He was happy about that. Turning to the left, he entered an overgrown formerly gravel driveway. Now, it was mostly dry grass with ruts. He used to have a home up here with his family of men. Men who did horrible things and brought the evidence here to get rid of it. Lane let them use his spot for a while and then asked them to move on. It was getting crowded. They left and Lane had not looked them up to get reacquainted.

Lane was back in the tree line again, and there was barely enough room for his car. Absently, he wondered if he should leave it alone. Driving here would reveal that someone had been her recently. He didn't stop. If no one came in a few days, the evidence of his passage would begin to disappear. He was a gambler and thought it was worth the risk.

When he could go no further with the car, Lane stopped and turned off the car. He pushed his door open enough to wiggle out and hoped he didn't have to come here again, ever. He just needed to verify the safety of the field.

Lane forced his way through the brush and felt it scratching his hands. He put his hands in his pockets and logged it away to put his gloves on before leaving the car if this ever happened

Bobbie Kaald

again. Soon, the bushes started to thin and get shorter. Next thing was a field with the beginnings of undergrowth.

Lane looked around and saw that there were a lot of dead trees. Dead trees were not good. This was a forest fire waiting to happen kind of stuff. A forest fire could and would result in his graveyard being discovered. Time to move on. He would leave the graves but move on for the last part of his life. His hideaway was a long way from here, but he was uncomfortable with his identity being revealed if this property were discovered.

"Dammit all. I'm definitely too old for this." Lane returned to his car and slowly began backing out. If he hit something, there would be minimal damage at this speed. He could not see where to go, but he drove by remote most of the time and this was no different.

Back on the gravel again, Lane continued to back up until he found a place to do a three-point turn around. This old car could barely do a three-point turn. If he had to, he would do a five-point turn for safety. His shoulders were stiff from all the driving and his arthritis, but he slowly made the turn and began driving back to the paved road.

"Time to go visit some of the old haunts." Lane spoke aloud to prevent himself from changing him mind. He thought about finding that off the path lake campground for now. He could lay his sleeping bag on the ground there and at least stretch out.

Finding the Family of Killers

When Lane reached the paved road, he turned toward Hiway two. It was the most direct road to the north and south road which would eventually lead to Canada. He drove through the night and arrived at the turn off just before dawn. As he drove north in the direction of the campground, a car passed him with a vaguely familiar older man driving but neither man stopped. He couldn't be certain who it was and wouldn't risk it not being him.

Lane drove past the lower campground because there was a car parked there. Curiously, there wasn't any tent. Taking the left, Lane found a spot in the trees because the shade would keep it cooler for longer. Turning the car off, Lane got out and walked around to the trunk. When he opened it, a stale odor came out and he shut it again. He needed a laundromat. The driver's door was still open, and Lane climbed back inside to make himself comfortable for some sleep. This was turning out to be a nightmare trip for him. When he woke up, he would find a laundry of some sort somewhere.

Bobbie Kaald

The Hunt

Michael and Roberts stopped for the night at the turn off to Lake Wenatchee. It would be cold, but they were too tired to continue driving safely.

When they stopped, Michael crawled into the back seat and handed Roberts a sleeping bag to keep warm. It took a bit to undo the sleeping bag but finally Michael was covered from chin to toe and beginning to warm-up. He never knew how long it took to warm up because the next thing he knew, Roberts was driving, and the sun was long up.

"Good morning, sleepy head. We will be in town soon. Do you have any idea where he would go? He has money and could

Finding the Family of Killers

book a room somewhere. I thought we would drive around town and watch for his car." Roberts kept his eyes on the road as he talked to let Michel wake up.

"I need coffee, first." Michael pulled Roberts open sleeping bag into the back with a lot of effort, and then crawled up into the passenger seat. He tried not to interfere with the driving.

"Hey, be careful." Roberts was laughing but the car swerved and fishtailed barely missing some oncoming traffic.

"Sorry, I was trying to be careful." Michael's heart was in his throat and he could barely speak. Flashes of his past came to him as if he were still there and he broke out into a cold sweat.

"Are you alright? I'm sorry that my maneuver I scared you." Roberts prepared to pull off if he needed to.

"I will be fine. How are we going to find Wolfe? Do we need to find Wolfe? I know his father is concerned but really, he is a man now and not on parole." Michael turned to face Roberts who had helped him so much, but he was very aware that he remained on parole under James.

"I'm not certain that we can or should find Wolfe, but for James sake mostly, I said that we would do it. Wolfe, Sr. is mostly concerned for his wife's sake." Roberts slowed as his car drove into town. "You look for Wolfe's car. I need to watch traffic. These tourists never look before they move." Roberts drove slowly through town and took a right. He planned to cover all the streets slowly and methodically. This would take all day and they would be lucky to make Wenatchee by bedtime.

Bobbie Kaald

It is a good thing this is one of the small towns. He found himself wishing for his travel account. This trip would take a long time to pay off on his credit card.

Finding the Family of Killers

A New Player

Zeke had been on his own for many years. He ran away from a man he knew as Tory. Tory killed Zeke's parents and found him hiding under his bed. Tory didn't kill little children, or so he said when he offered him a ride to his grand-parent's house.

Tory lied. After he got Zeke out from under his bed. Tory put a hand over his mouth and picked him up. He carried him in such a way that Zeke didn't see his parents as they left the house. Zeke never saw his parents again and at that moment, Tory named him Zeke. He no longer remembered his old name, or where he used to live. He never saw his grandparents.

Bobbie Kaald

Zeke stayed with Tory for many years, later he listened to things he heard when Tory and Sam would talk. He helped keep the place clean and never went to school. No one knew he lived with Tory and no one from the outside ever saw him.

Zeke was standing in the window with Sam when Bill killed that poor orphan girl for no reason. Sam had gasped and Zeke wet himself but left the house on a run and never looked back. He hid during the day and ran at night for years. He ate when he found it and used trees for his bathroom.

When he found his first abandoned house, he moved right inside. He slept the sleep of the dead that night and every night since then. He stayed in that house for nearly five years alone in the cold darkness of the moldy house until someone came and claimed the property was theirs. He moved out before the new owners even came inside.

All that was long behind him. He had streaks of gray in his hair now and still wondered at why he had become just like Bill whenever he saw a young girl. Zeke really saw the first sweet young thing who walked between him and a tree one day when he just lost another job. His anger boiled out of him the second he saw that little girl who never did a thing to him. His vision turned white and the next thing he knew that little girl lay on the ground next to that tree.

The rest of the week was lost to Zeke's memory. All he could remember was that girl laying on her side at the base of the tree.

Finding the Family of Killers

She looked so like that lost orphan girl that he shivered every time she came to his mind, a ghost from his past.

Zeke's life was nearly over now. He rarely got angry, but that didn't stop him from occasionally helping a little girl go missing. They were all buried out in his back yard with plants that he bought to commemorate their passing.

This was Zeke's real problem. There was a drought this year and he was not allowed to water the plants. All his work would die this year if he weren't lucky. If luck prevailed, only half of it would die. Any which way he looked at it, he needed to move on before his little garden was littered with the bones he knew to be there.

Sighing, Zeke turned and walked back through his house for the last time. His car was already packed with everything that he needed to take. He was tired of his well-used furniture and felt happy to leave it behind. A new adventure at this phase of his life was not something he ever expected to happen.

Zeke got into his car and turned the ignition. It sputtered more than a little before bursting into life. "Stay with me baby." Zeke was not ready to get a new car because he was probably going to start stealing them. "This is a rough way to live for an old man." He drove away thinking about that newspaper article a while back about Bill hanging in a tree off the Mountain Pass Hiway.

Bobbie Kaald

Bitter Reunion

Anyone in the know would think the moon was full and mercury was aligned in the great conjunction. All of the family of killers were once again on the prowl. All except Michael, who was hunting for a former recruit who was on the run from life. Of course, Wolfe was not hunting. He was hiding.

Tory passed Wolfe unknowingly and was headed south. He let the car choose the road and found himself at the Dry Falls visitor center. He like the Dry Falls and the Grand Canyon but at least at the Dry Falls he could breathe and not have to change his shirt every two minutes because he was soaked with sweat.

Finding the Family of Killers

Tory walked slowly along the edge of the Dry Falls. It had a very stunning and peaceful beauty that he only appreciated because it allowed him a place to get out and stretch. When others were present, he mimicked them as he did in his entire life. There were many things that he simply did not understand because he had no feelings.

Entering the visitor center, Tory wandered past all the displays and pretended to read them as he did whenever he stopped. He read them once a long time ago and they were interesting, but he had no need to rehash old times.

Tory stopped and bought a postcard just to make it look like he was a real tourist. He smiled and nodded at the cashier before turning to walk back out to his car. He stopped to use the facility and left the postcard in the trash can under his paper towels.

Tory was nearly to his car when another car drove in and almost ran him over. His temper was already on edge and he started screaming. "Are you crazy! I'm walking here!" He would have said more but he suddenly recognized the driver and his anger dissipated as if he was never out of control.

The car's brakes screamed and came to a stop just touching Tory's pants. Wolfe jumped out before thinking. "I am so sorry. Did I hit you or hurt you?" Just as Tory recognized Wolfe, Wolfe recognized Tory.

"How have you been, son?" Tory asked and smiled. "We haven't seen each other for a very long time."

Bobbie Kaald

Wolfe started backing up to return to his car without taking his eyes off Tory. The wind chose that second to gust through the parking lot and blow dirt up into everyone's eyes. Wolfe jumped in and started to back up, having not turned off his car.

Before Wolfe could relock the car, Tory opened the door and was in. "Let's go and have lunch. You can leave alone after that or just drop me off in town."

Wolfe didn't want to eat with Tory. He didn't want him in his car. He didn't answer Tory, but just waited for him to get in and buckle up before driving south to find a place to eat as requested. Wolfe remained silent for the duration of the drive, but his brain was winding up faster and faster as he tried to decide what to do.

Tory started off talking about everything under the sun as a means of helping Wolfe to relax. After about twenty minutes, he stopped talking and resolved to enjoy the ride and part ways again when they arrived in town.

Wolfe drove along the river and eventually into town. He hated driving through this busy country city. Taking the first turn off, he drove down the old main street of the city. It looked nearly abandoned as did many town centers across America.

"Drop me off at any food establishment." Tory said this to let Wolfe know he did not have to eat with him. He would not want to eat with an associate of his kidnapper.

Finding the Family of Killers

Wolfe did not acknowledge the comment. He saw a place about a block away and pulled into it and stopped in the center of the parking lot.

"Thanks for the ride. Good to see you again." Tory remained cordial with his conversation. He may need this relationship in the future. Opening the door, Tory got out and shut the door. He stepped away just in time.

Wolfe was so petrified that he spun the tires in his rush to get away from Tory. The tires screamed and smoked leaving wide snaking black marks from his passing. Maybe leaving home was not a good idea. He was already driving west, but he slowed to the speed limit because he didn't want a ticket. Continuing to drive west, Wolfe did his best to calm himself down. By the time he reached the short pass heading south, Wolfe decided not to go home just yet.

Wolfe turned into the left turn lane and waited his chance. Headed south, Wolfe now felt much calmer. He didn't know how many men he was avoiding but he had to get away at least for now. Later, maybe he would go home.

Bobbie Kaald

Missed Again

Roberts and Michael drove out of the first town after an unsuccessful search about thirty minutes ago. Roberts planned to drive to the large town coming up and rent a room. Stopping for the light, he watched as a car turned and head south. Looking over, Michael was asleep.

Driving straight ahead, Roberts had only his own thoughts for the thirty-minute drive. He might make it without falling asleep. In the morning, he would talk it over with Michael and probably head home. This trip was pointless. Wolfe could be anywhere in the state and they would never find him. A thousand officers would be hard put to find him.

Finding the Family of Killers

James probably put out a missing person report by now. This would help more than anything Roberts could do now that he was retired.

Happy with his decision, Roberts drove down the long newly widened road trying his darnedest not to fall asleep. He needed a candy bar to tide him through until dinner. He didn't have one. Staying awake when all others were snoring was always difficult. Rolling down his window about a third of the way, Roberts kept driving and hoped the cool night air would be enough to keep his brain clear and his eyes open.

It was a monotonous drive. Agent Roberts tried to watch the hillsides although some of them were cliff sides. Rarely did he see a new construction. This was a place out of time as far as Roberts was concerned. Most of the buildings having been in existence since the late nineteen-fifties or before. This is the main reason he had so much difficulty staying awake. His police radio took the place of a musical radio and he could not even listen to the depressing country western music that blared from ninety-nine percent of the stations.

At last, Roberts approached the town. He made a left at the first motel he found. They could walk to eat or have it delivered. "Michael, wake up because we have arrived. You really need to get a license."

"I know, but I can just take the bus." Michael and Roberts were both occupied with getting out and stretching. Which is

Bobbie Kaald

too bad because Tory was behind them getting into an unlocked car.

About the time Michael and Roberts entered the motel lobby, Tory drove out of the parking lot heading west because you can only make a right turn out of the parking lot.

"Hey, stop that car. That man stole my car!" A man at the counter yelled and pointed.

"Call the police and tell them a retired FBI agent is in pursuit." Roberts left to get back into his car. Michael followed behind him with reluctance. He wanted to eat.

When Roberts got the car started, he noticed that he didn't have much gas. "I hope a local meets us because we can't go far with this little amount of gas." With that, he turned on his police radio and left the parking lot with his foot pushing the gas pedal to the floor. He could barely see the other car a good half mile down the road just disappearing around the first corner.

Roberts and Michael never caught sight of the car again. He was forced to pull off at an exit to the highway and double back. He called it in and then returned to town. This time, he pulled into a gas station first and filled up the tank. After that they went back and rented a room, leaving the car at the motel, they walked to the restaurant for dinner.

While they were waiting to eat, a local police officer came in and took their statements. They discussed how a man stole a car. None of them could be absolutely certain they recognized

Finding the Family of Killers

the driver as Tory. For this reason, they only gave the general vague and unhelpful descriptions of the man from his back.

"Sorry to be of little to no assistance, but we lost him at the first turn. He might not have stayed on the main road after that. I didn't anticipate him turning off so soon." Roberts said and shook hands with the officer because his food had arrived, and he was ravenously hungry.

"Glad for the heads up. I have my men searching. He will undoubtedly abandon his car somewhere and we will be back to the beginning. I will message your local police if we come up with something." The officer turned to leave but stopped when Michael spoke up.

"We are looking for my friend, Wolfe. He has west coast plates and took a trip. We are concerned for his mental condition. If you find him, just tell him to give us a call." Michael smiled when he finished and noted the officer nodded that he received his message. The officer turned and walked outside.

After eating dinner in silence, Roberts and Michael walked back over to their room and laydown without undressing. Their sleep was short lived due to multiple trains going by during the night. Finally, at around three in the morning. Roberts woke up Michael and told him they were leaving. Roberts made a mental note not to bother with a motel room if there were railroad tracks near-by in the future.

Roberts waited in the car for Michael to arrive. He was too tired to go home but he couldn't sleep and just wanted to get

Bobbie Kaald

on the way. Michael finally arrived and his door barely shut before Roberts was backing out and moving quickly through the parking lot full of cars but devoid of life.

"What's the rush?" Michael asked with genuine concern.

"Try to stay awake because your job is to keep me awake. By the way, you are getting a learner's permit when we get home because I am too old to do all the driving." Roberts thought of Michael like the son he never had and felt guilty for letting this part of Michael's life slip through the cracks.

Four hours later, Roberts parked poorly in front of his home. "Michael, we're home. You might as well go to work and fill James in because you slept all the way there and all the way home. Thanks for keeping me awake." Roberts spoke with a voice heavy with sleep and sarcasm. He got out and slammed his door shut. Two minutes later, he was asleep on his bed, fully dressed in the black oblivion of dreamless sleep.

Finding the Family of Killers

Family Reunion

Once Zeke got on the road, his mind began to wander. He remembered that he still owned an abandoned warehouse near the infamous Sun Lakes. Relaxing slowly but methodically as he headed for his selected destination, Zeke's camera mind began flashing across his life at the warehouse.

As Zeke recalled, he buried some of his first victims in the dirt floor and then covered it with a regular floor. He needed to go and check on the building condition again. He made trips by there every few years and opened it up to verify the building was still in acceptable shape. The windows were boarded up when he left the first time and he ran the furnace set at a low

Bobbie Kaald

temperature to prevent freezing and pipe damage, even though the water was disconnected.

Zeke knew the warehouse wasn't really at Sun Lakes, but he just found it easier to remember if he thought that. It was really on the outskirts of Coulee City. They put on a nice light display on the fourth of July every year. It was well past the fourth, but it was a nice memory, of which he had few.

When he drove past the entrance to the State Park, there was a barrier blocking entrance to it. Zeke couldn't help himself, he turned around and drove back. Stopping next to the sign, he read it quickly and then laughed so hard he had tears in his eyes. It was closed due to earwig infestation. It would be closed for another week to let the insecticide dissipate.

Zeke turned the car around and continued driving toward his warehouse. His smile spread across his face and remained on his face and inside of his soul. He knew about the earwigs and had known for many years, but no one did anything. DDT was a horrid pesticide because it killed the entire planet in its own way. Nothing really killed earwigs or cockroaches.

Zeke tried not to watch the roadside because he found it depressing this time of the year. Dead grass so dry that a small increase in the heat and a spark from a spun tire could and did set off a fire that would burn unabated for hours or days or longer.

Finding the Family of Killers

Turning to the right, Zeke drove south as the sun quickly set behind the mountains. He didn't turn on his lights because he made a sharp left into a gravel road and headed into his own unpopulated backcountry environment. Without his lights on, he needed to drive at a slow crawl and weaving in between the sagebrush as straight ahead as he was able. From his memory of many years ago, this is where he thought that he should go.

As it turns out, lights would have been a good idea. About ten minutes into the drive, he ran into the building, literally. Slamming on his brakes, belatedly, Zeke turned off the car. "I'm home." He said and laughed. This was not the first time this had happened.

Zeke got out of the car and walked around to the front of this week's car. As he passed the edge of his car, he reached out and touched the wall of the warehouse. Turning to the left, Zeke took a couple of steps and then returned to his car for a flashlight.

Turning on the light, Zeke cupped his hand over the lens and only let out a small amount of light. He had done this many times as a way of preventing most of the light from going a great distance. He walked slowly due to plant growth from the last time he had been here. It was short and stubby sagebrush and without seeing it, he knew there was dead grass underneath because it crunched when he walked.

Reaching the door, Zeke turned off the flashlight and shoved it into a pocket because the door took two hands. Flipping the

Bobbie Kaald

latch, he gripped the handle in both hands and leaned against the latch to make the old-rusted door move. He was instantly sorry when it did move because it emitted a high-pitched squeal as the pulleys turned slightly. He stopped pulling and the noise stopped. Maybe it was enough. Zeke was just able to squeeze through, but he heard a short ripping sound as part of his clothing let him know how old it was and how much fatter than the opening he was.

Once inside, Zeke pulled out his flashlight, or torch as the English called it, and turned it on. He scanned the light around the warehouse. It remained as before, empty except for leaves and dirt and spiderwebs. He also heard many small somethings running around. If he had to guess, rats or something worse.

The floor was untouched and remained intact. This is why Zeke came today. He was too old to stay here and turned to leave. He doused the light and pushed on the door a little more before leaving. He had no trouble getting through the space this time and turned to shut the sliding door. Putting all of his might behind pulling the door shut was nearly not enough. With an ear-piercing scream, the door slid shut and Zeke fell backward onto the ground beside his car.

"I will bring oil the next time I come, or maybe WD-40." Zeke mumbled to himself. If he were his younger self, he probably would have been cursing a lot using multiple vulgar sentiments. Pulling himself up by the door handle, Zeke felt the handle groan

Finding the Family of Killers

softly and let go of it. All he needed was for the handle to pull off the door.

Sighing, loudly, Zeke opened the car door gently and got back inside. This was the only thing on his list of to do items before moving on. It was done now and he started the car to head for parts unknown.

Bobbie Kaald

Grand Coulee

Lane drove all night and he was tired. Night driving was not something that he should be doing because his vision was going, and the glare of the headlights obliterated everything in front of him. When he saw a park was coming up, he thought he would risk having to pay to camp. Just one night wouldn't break him.

Entering the camp, he turned off his lights and slowed to a crawl. He drove around looking for an empty spot and found one at the very back. Pulling in and turning off the car, Lane fell asleep before he could even get out.

Finding the Family of Killers

Lane slept until dawn and got out of his car to relieve himself and unkink his old bones that cracked like a breakfast cereal when he stood up. There were too many cars for him to be crass and use a bush. He hurried to the community facility to find a urinal. As he walked along at a hurried rate, he passed a car that brought back memories of his past life. A smile crossed his face as pictures of the past played across his internal screen. He had mixed feelings about those memories, but with a more urgent need to contend with he turned his mind back to finding his goal of a urinal in which to relieve himself.

When Lane returned, the car was driving away. He caught a glimpse of an older man with grayish hair behind the wheel. It was not a good enough look for recognition, but his thoughts were on other things.

When he reached his car, Lane slowly sat down behind the wheel and shut the door. He started it up and headed for the local gasoline station. It was several miles into the town and a couple more to find the station. Lane was glad he did not push the limit of his fuel before stopping or he would have run out of gas before pulling into the station.

Driving through the tiny older town, Lane thought it was just the same as the last time he visited many years ago. He did see a few houses that were recently painted at least. The old feeling of restlessness settled over Lane. He really hated small towns and wanted to get into a larger city. He never felt that he belonged anywhere. He was just hiding, always hiding.

Bobbie Kaald

As Lane pulled into the gas station, he saw the very same car pulled up to the pumps that he saw in the campground. Pulling in from the opposite direction, Lane stopped his car and turned off the engine. As he got out, he saw an older man leaning on the other car as he held the nozzle into the gas tank access.

"Excuse me, I saw you earlier and wanted to tell you that I really love that car of yours." Lane was still talking when the man interrupted him.

"I saw you. That's why I left while you were pissing your heart out in the latrine. I wanted to tell you that you may not steal my car because I already stole it from you years ago." Zeke didn't turn around because he was watching the pump. He had been right to leave early but wrong that the man would not possibly come this direction.

Lane dropped his mouth open when the man spoke so to him. Stolen, his car had been stolen from him years ago by a man named Zeke. A member of his little group of men that he used to run with. "You must be kidding. A man named Zeke stole my car from me, years ago."

"You're catching on, Lane." Zeke hung up his pump handle because he was finished. "I'm going down to the dam for a little breakfast. See you there." Zeke got into his car, having paid in advance, and drove away without looking Lane in the eye.

Lane was speechless but his hose clicked off just then. He put the nozzle away and replaced the gas cap and headed inside to

Finding the Family of Killers

pay for his purchase. This gave him a chance to decide if it was worth following Zeke and reactivating his instincts. How did that old man know his name? Could he be Zeke? Impossible!

By the time he was back in his car, Lane decided that he needed to know the answer. He sighed heavily knowing that this was high up in the rank of the worst decisions that he ever made in his life. Starting the car up, he drove out of the station and turned toward the dam.

Bobbie Kaald

Soffia

Soffia knew that Roberts and Michael returned from their unsuccessful mission of mercy late last night. James received a call and she always woke up from the obnoxiously loud ringing piercing her brain. She lay awake late into the night after that and eventually got up and left James a note to invite the two bachelors to dinner.

As Soffia prepared her ill fated meal, she hoped that Natasha and Helena would not show up. Fate usually wasn't on her side and because of that, she prepared extra. The girls were still nervous around Michael and she watched his face the last time they were together. Michael was equally nervous around them.

Finding the Family of Killers

Hearing a car drive up outside, Soffia went to look and as she suspected, the girls just arrived. Soffia sighed and went to greet the girls. Everything would be okay. Maybe the boys were too tired to come but Michael was always hungry. She didn't think he ate very well when he was a captive.

Soffia unlocked the door and opened it. She intended to wait for the girls but remembered that dinner was probably burning. Returning to the kitchen it crossed her mind that James would not like her leaving the door unlocked and open.

"Mom, why is the door open?" Natasha's voice came from the open door followed by the sound of the door shutting and being locked as she spoke.

Soffia was sad to have to begin locking her door after all the years of just shutting it. The discovery of the body by Natasha changed all of that forever. "I'm in here. Did I miss your call?"

"I'm sorry. I didn't call. We were out shopping and ended up extremely close to here. You don't mind drop-ins for dinner, do you?" Natasha came around the corner into the kitchen as she spoke, and Helena wandered down to use the bathroom before there was anyone else in there. Houses built in the year this one was rarely had more than one bathroom.

"I might as well tell you that James is inviting Roberts and Michael to come for dinner. They returned late last night from their unsuccessful search for Wolfe." Soffia was ready to dish up but just turned the food off. If she turned it down, it would burn anyway. "We need to set the table for more people."

Bobbie Kaald

With the three women changing the table around, the table was set before anyone else arrived. "Should we call to see if they will be late?" Natasha asked and then laughed as she heard cars arriving outside. "I think we can dish up. Maybe put it on the plates so the women get their fair share."

Soffia smiled at the idea of dishing onto the plates and did it for the first time in her life. Mostly, she just wanted to see what James would say.

After everyone finished eating, Soffia brought out a rare and exotic dessert, rarely served except at Thanksgiving. Pumpkin pie was a favorite of hers and she kept some frozen for times when nothing else said celebration in quite the same way.

Michael's eyes bugged out of his head and his jaw dropped open. "Wow." It was all that he could say, and it covered his feelings about being served this delicacy.

"I think that you forgot to ask for whipping cream." James was not expecting this and remembered that she always asked for whipping cream.

"Not to worry, I walked down and got some. The exercise is good for me, except for coming back up the hill." Soffia was still smiling.

Natasha stood up and helped with dishing up. "We can cut it into six pieces and then no one needs to fight over left-overs."

Finding the Family of Killers

"Way ahead of you." Soffia had it divided and six plates for the pieces. "You do the whipping cream. I already whipped it. Just a little more and then add the special ingredients."

"Yes, mom. I know how to do it." Natasha and her mom kept these two ingredients secret from the men and she went over to the stove to finish the whipping cream. What she was doing could not be seen by those at the table. When she finished, she brought the bowl over and put a heaping spoonful onto each piece. Smiling, she took Helena and her piece over and sat back down. It was a lot of fun to slowly torture the men who were practically drooling.

Helena watched Natasha and Soffia tease the rest of them. It made her smile and feel grateful for being part of this adopted family. She loved coming here for dinner and entertainment.

James waited for everyone to finish their desert before nodding at Roberts to reveal his news. He dreaded letting him tell the women, but with Helena here it could be done all at the same time.

Roberts cleared his throat and swallowed the last of his cooled coffee before making his news announcement. "I think everyone knows that we did not find Wolfe when we were in Eastern Washington. What you don't know is that Michael and I recognized Tory. We gave chase but lost him. The local force is still searching for him."

"Tory?" Helena asked. She had difficulty remembering the names.

Bobbie Kaald

"Tory is the man who I lived with most of the time. Sam killed my mother, but Sam also killed himself." Michael was still slowly eating the pie. He savored every smidgen. It was rare that he had homemade food, and only at James and Soffia's.

This brought silence from all those present. Finally, Helena spoke. "Natasha, I think that we should be going."

"Thanks for dinner. Helena's right, we need to leave. We have been gone all day." Natasha spoke with her mom as they followed Helena to the door. Then, Natasha turned and left. Helena was already half-way to the car.

Michael stood behind Soffia. "I'm sorry, Soffia. I shouldn't have come." He turned and went to sit on the couch out of the way. Roberts would wait for the girls to leave. They didn't want them to feel like they were being followed.

Finding the Family of Killers

Tory

Tory drove slowly through town with his heart pounding in his chest for several hours. He recognized Michael and the man with him from the day Sam killed himself and Michael defected. It had been a long time, but Michael looked just the same as the last time he saw him.

Just as they saw Tory, the car engine turned over on the car he was stealing. The owner had nicely left the keys in the lock and that is why he was stealing this particular car. It started right up. Driving by remote, Tory flew out of the parking lot and headed west on the main road. He would have gone east but there was an island in the center of the road and his car would have dropped the drive shaft if he tried to jump the island.

Bobbie Kaald

His heart was pounding in his chest, and Tory was afraid it would give out. Deciding at the last second, Tory turned right without signaling, and left the main road. He hoped this move was unobserved by the authorities. As luck would have it, no one followed him. He slowed to twenty miles an hour as a way of allowing his anxiety to dissipate to a tolerable level.

That was several hours ago, and Tory just stayed on the city streets since then. He drove past a cemetery about ten minutes ago and was now driving out of the city into the desolate dry grass area that surrounded what passed for civilization here on the Eastern side of the Mountains. Forest fire or grass fire, it didn't matter. They were all too common of problems because it rarely rained in the summer over here.

Tory didn't know what time it was. The clock in this piece of junk car was broken. This eventually happened in older cars before the age of digital clocks. However, it was easier to steal an older car and people didn't care or report older car thefts as often. He would change up this car for another older car soon.

Tory had a sudden thought. He would head for the junkyard and see if the police impounded it or not. Bill put his real name and four other names on the purchase of the property deed. Any one of them could pay the property tax, in fact, anyone can pay the property tax. No one would pay property taxes if they

Finding the Family of Killers

didn't own the property, but it is just something that Tory always thought about.

'Yes, I need to go to the junkyard. I can change cars there.' Tory thought to himself. He suddenly had to stop the car in the middle of the road. This was a dead-end, he needed to turn around.

Cursing creatively, Tory turned around and drove back to his last turn. He decided to stop these shenanigans drive back into town and head for the pass. It was dark and there was no traffic here to follow as a way of finding the main road to the highway. A main road would have some traffic, but he would keep his speed down. With any luck, the police were at coffee break.

Laboriously, Tory wandered back to the main road and drove along until all of the main roads merged into the highway. This town was laid out in the haphazard fashion of a farm town that grew into a major town of consequence. Reaching the highway merge, Tory sat at the light and waited impatiently for it to turn. He did not want to attract the attention of an unseen city cruiser by turning on a red light.

Finally, the light turned green and Tory made his legal left turn and was on his way west. As he passed the restaurant where he stole this car, he started watching his review mirror for a mile or two to see if he was being followed. No head lights appeared behind him and he began to relax just a little.

Tory found the radio was tuned to a local station when he turned it on for a distraction. He turned on the heat and tried

Bobbie Kaald

to use it. It was working but the fan was broken. He turned it off. After swerving more than a little, Tory stopped playing with the dials. If he needed help staying awake, he could roll down the window halfway. If it didn't rain, that is.

Tory must have zoned off because he nearly missed his turn. Without looking in his rear-view mirror, Tory braked hard and swerved to the left. His tires squealed a little and he fishtailed a lot. With great difficulty, he maintained his forward direction without doing a donut. This was the big drawback to an older car. They all had rear wheel drive and tended to be difficult to control in a slide.

"I got to stop doing that." Tory spoke aloud in an angry voice as his heart pounded in his chest and ears. He sighed deeply a couple of times before relaxing again. Smiling at his own repeat stupidity, he continued driving along for a short distance before pulling over onto a pullout.

Tory opened the door after he stopped the car, but the car rolled. He slammed it into park and applied the emergency brake. Next time he even thought about stealing a Ford, he would not comply with his urge or just shoot himself. Laughing at his foolishness, he opened the door.

Tory got out and stretched his aching old bones hoping that the cracking he heard would relieve some of his back pain. He walked toward the far side of the pull out into the darkness and

Finding the Family of Killers

urinated quickly. He did not need to have this all end with an arrest for urinating in public and indecent exposure.

Walking back to his car, Tory got inside and slammed the door. Starting the car back up, he noticed the gas gauge was at half. He thought it was full enough to make the run and pulled back onto the road heading south. He planned to find another car at the other end of the pass.

Bobbie Kaald

Junkyard

Tory arrived at the Junkyard turn off just before dawn. He turned and drove slowly with his lights off, as he always did. This time though, Tory stopped the car and turned it off. He got out and left the door open. He would walk and make as little noise as possible.

Tory walked slower than he ever had before because he was getting old and now became short of breath if he walked too fast. Even walking slowly, Tory needed several breaks to rest up enough to reach the gate.

Along the way, Tory heard no noises. An occasional animal sound as they voiced their needs into the night air. Thankfully,

Finding the Family of Killers

there was only minimal wind and what dust was kicked up remained low. As he reached the gate, a light rain began to fall.

Tory stood at the gate for a long time. Everything appeared to be the same, and there was no sign of life. Taking off the necklace holding the gate key, Tory unlocked the gate and pulled it open. Cursing his paranoia, Tory began his walk back to the car that he could have driven all the way up to the gate.

Eventually, Tory reached his car and shook the water off as much as he was able to before getting in. As he entered the car, his hand touched a seat covered with water. It pooled because he left the door open. "Paranoia consequences, you old fool." Tory spoke aloud to himself because there was no one else there to witness his stupidity. He shook his head and sat on the puddle of water because he was already soaking wet, and this car would be crushed as soon as he was able to.

It took a couple of tries, but Tory started the car and drove up to the gate. This only took a minute or so because the sun was coming up and a legally blind man could see the way.

Stopping the car just inside of the gate, Tory got out to shut the gate but stopped in his tracks as another car began approaching him with the lights off. He waited because no mater who it was, they obviously had been here before.

The approaching car stopped just shy of the gate to turn into the junkyard. Presumedly, they stopped to open the gate. The

Bobbie Kaald

driver's window rolled down and an old man's face looked out. "You ain't Bill, cause he's dead. Who are you? You got a key so you must have knew Bill."

"I did know Bill, but as you say, he is dead. And, just who are you, two?" Tory added the two because another old man just sat up in the backseat.

"I'm Zeke, and I brought along Lane because we had to dump his car in case it was still on the sheets from long ago." Zeke answered Tory as if he were always friendly to people he just met, but he barely remembered how to be civil after all of these years. "Why don't you drive on up and we will shut the gate and then follow you?"

Tory was still suspicious but nodded in agreement and returned to his car for the drive up to the small building. The number of cars left on the site decreased immensely the last time he visited here with Bill. Bill sold off all of the crushed cars and that gave them money for some time. With Bill's death, his share would never be recovered.

Tory drove up to the back of the house because his car needed stripping and crushing. Stolen recently, it was too hot to drive any longer. Getting out of his car, Tory walked around the building and saw two men get out of Zeke's car. They appeared to be near Bill's age, whatever that was. "Bill helped raise me. How did you know Bill?" He still needed to continue the conversation and find the unspoken answers.

Finding the Family of Killers

Lane laughed as did Zeke. "We all have a lot in common. None of us are related, and we all learned from Bill or someone else to be sociable and murderous." Lane turned and looked at Tory as he tried to decide who this man was with a key to the yard.

Tory turned and entered the building. It was never locked. There was nothing in it worth stealing. Being the first to enter, he took the most comfortable chair, even though he was the youngest. The other two men followed him inside and made themselves as comfortable as they were able to.

"I have thought a lot about this place over the years. With all the advancements, I'm not certain about keeping this place. Not to mention that it involves laborious work that's hard on the back." Zeke started off the discussion.

"It is a convenient place for disposing of vehicles that are on the sheets." Tory said but had been thinking the same thing.

"That it is, but I don't think it is safe to stay here. It would be good to get it up working again. If any authorities show up, we will know that the place is burned." Lane spoke his piece.

"Might be a good idea, and then we can crush up the cars we need disposed of and some of the others that are still sitting around. I can call our scrap buyer and ask if he has anything needing to be compacted." Tory revealed part of the reason that he had come here. "We need an inventory of supplies, gasoline and the like. It hasn't been too long since I witnessed

Bobbie Kaald

the crusher working. Maybe we need to change the oil, but not much else. After that, we need a car that isn't hot."

Lane and Zeke agreed. The three men had a plan and would cruise the town tonight when they went in for dinner. Slow was the word and it would keep them as safe as they could be. All of them were old enough to take their time with their wicked cravings. The men all fell asleep after making the plan from the exhaustion of their trip here. Later, they would slowly begin the next step of their plan.

Finding the Family of Killers

Missing

Michael remained high powered and vigilant from his years of captivity. He constantly obsessed about doing things just the right way as a way of assuring himself that he would not be punished. Consciously, he knew that James and Roberts didn't mind an occasional mistake. It was Michael who could not bear making a mistake.

Michael felt this extreme guilt over the deaths that Tory and Sam had caused. He didn't really know about Isaac's and Bill was dead. He kept a careful file for his own use containing copies of any fax of a missing child. Young boys were in one file and females of any age went in another file. He also added unsolved female murder victims to the female file.

Bobbie Kaald

James knew about these files and hoped that it would help Michael come to grips with his feelings. Also, James thought another set of eyes might help to find something that others missed.

Michael had been keeping these files since he first got back and began helping James. That was more than two years ago. As Michael approached the end of his probation, the number of faxes on missing young people began to increase. This worried Michael but James didn't seem concerned or at least he didn't show his concern.

Michael just collected the missing persons posters and copied them for his own files. After he filed the official posters, Michael took his copies over to the area where he worked. He did his daily routine of sorting and adding to the folders. After this, he counted the posters in each folder. Today there was one that didn't fit anywhere.

Michael thought it was just a missing woman's flier until he read it closely enough to file it. As he read, his hands began to shake and his eyes dripped tears down his cheeks unheeded by him. "James. James!" He kept repeating this louder and louder until James was by his side shaking him to get him to answer.

Finding the Family of Killers

"Michael snap out of it and tell me what you found." James didn't yell but spoke in a firm tone of voice to try to get Michael to respond to the question in an intelligible fashion.

"They're back." Michael's voice was soft, and his answer was short and crisp. He handed James the flier before sitting down on James extra chair. He grabbed a bottle of water from the case on the floor by his chair and drank most of it quickly.

James took the flier from Michael but continued to stare at the paleness of his parolee. "I have some news for you." He did not look at the flier. "The new DA called and has terminated your parole. You are a citizen again, for the third time." Michael was never charged with anything. His parole was more or less a kind of witness protection, from himself.

"Really good timing then." Michael had begun to sweat and didn't look relieved at all.

This did not slip by James unnoticed, but it spurred him into looking at the flier. "Okay, I see that a woman was found dead. Reportedly, her son is missing. No relative admits to having him and the father died previously." Apparently, James wasn't taking this seriously enough because Michael jumped up and flew at him.

"*The boy is missing.* Don't you get it. Someone has the boy and is teaching him about killing." Michael banged his fists on James desk and then flew out of the office and the station.

James picked up the phone and called Roberts. "It's James. The worst has finally happened. Michael found a flier like when

Bobbie Kaald

he was abducted." James listened and then added. "A boy is missing," more listening, "he's gone for a run. I'm just finishing up." James hung up and stood up to go make copies of this flier. He would hang some up around town and Roberts would need to travel with him to the very same town where they found remains in that ghost town, eventually.

Finding the Family of Killers

Disaster

In the ghost town, Wolfe pulled off to rest just at the front entrance and on the outside of the gate. He knew that this was not a good place to stop because of the past. However, he was too tired for caution. Rather than fall asleep at the wheel, he chose to stop here just before the metal gate. It was installed after Michael's group passed through, but a person could still walk inside if it remained closed. For some reason, it was open even though it was well past sunset, but Wolfe didn't want to get locked inside while he was asleep.

Wolfe stayed in his car and leaned back to let his body relax and sleep if he could. His mind was churning even more than when he left home. He felt like he was being chased most of the

Bobbie Kaald

way. When he turned to come this direction, the car behind him stayed on the main road allowing Wolfe to relax just a little.

Sometime later, Wolfe was mostly asleep but beginning to dream about a waterfall. He awakened slowly until he jolted awake with two realizations filling his brain. One was that he needed a nature call, and two was that someone was pounding on his car window.

Wolfe jumped and glared at the window and the person on the other side of it. After a long pause, he rolled the window down just a crack. "What?" He used his worst condescending voice reserved for the bullies in his life.

"Hi, my name is Lori. My date dumped me, and I saw your car sitting here. I mean, I just wondered if you could give me a ride to town." The girl with long black hair sporting many waves the full length of it smiled and cocked her head at a slight angle awaiting his answer.

Wolfe remembered what Michael told him about how he accidentally killed a girl. It started just like this. "No." He rolled up the window and started the car, thinking that was the end of the subject.

As Wolfe put the car into gear, Lori stepped in front of his car effectively blocking his exit. She put her hands on the hood of the car and leaned in. Wolfe stopped, threw it into reverse and gunned it. He stopped just shy of the gate into the actual ghost

Finding the Family of Killers

town. Putting the car back into drive, Wolfe headed for the road.

Lori remained where he left her. She looked woefully sad and Wolfe's heart burned with guilt. He drove around her and stopped at the exit. In the review mirror, Wolfe saw Lori slowly walking up behind him. No one was coming and Wolfe nearly pulled out, leaving Lori behind.

He looked into his review mirror again and watch the sad dejected figure walking toward the road. They were miles from anywhere and Wolfe just couldn't do it. He rolled down his window and motioned for her to hurry up, and then waved toward the passenger side. He glanced over and saw the door was locked.

Wolfe put the car into park and leaned over the long front seat. He barely reached the lock button and lifted it with his extended fingertip. Sitting up, Wolfe didn't have long to wait. The door opened and Lori slid inside.

"Thank you so much for the ride. I don't know what made you change your mind, but you won't be sorry." Lori spoke brokenly due to being breathless from the hundred-meter dash she just did. Her belongings were on the floor at her feet.

"I can only take you to the main road." Wolfe was already driving and vowed to himself never to come here again. Only bad things happened here, and he wouldn't be happy until 'Lori' left his car. He never wanted to see her again.

Bobbie Kaald

Lori sat next to him silently, nearly holding her breath. She worried that if she said anything, he would kick her out. She had been on her own for a few years and could pick up negativity from people fairly easily. This man was full of anger, but she was desperate. If she lived through this, she needed to change her ways.

Wolfe was nearing the main road and decided to see if she was going his way. "I am going to the right and there is a service station a couple of miles down the road. Would that be an okay place for you to get out? You might pick up another ride more easily there than out in the middle of nowhere."

Lori was surprised and shocked by the offer. "That will really be a great help to me. Thank-you." She could get another ride there and had done so in the past.

Wolfe needed to use the facilities and buy breakfast anyway. When he pulled into the parking lot, Wolfe turned off the car and they both got out. He saw Lori take her things out before closing the door. Wolfe locked the doors and made his way over to the entrance of the mini market. He would get gasoline at a later date. Entering quickly, Wolfe walked directly to the back and into the vacant men's room.

Wolfe exited only a bare two minutes later. He gathered a few items along the way. No customers were waiting at the cashier's and Wolfe paid for his nutritionally poor breakfast and took it with him to his car. As he walked out, Wolfe saw Lori

Finding the Family of Killers

talking to an extremely old man with fly away hair. Wolfe didn't know this was Zeke because he didn't know Zeke.

Bobbie Kaald

It Begins

Zeke returned to the little gas station. The prices were high but there were fewer people here to see him. When he got out to fill up the car, he leaned over more than usual and walked inside with cash to activate the pump. A young man was just paying, and Zeke slapped the cash down, "Everything on one." Walking back out he saw a woman with black wavy hair. He thought her so beautiful that he said so. "Hi there, beautiful. I can give you a ride as soon as I fill up."

Lori's head went up as soon as she heard the man's voice. He looked a lot like her grand-father, and she smiled at him. "I sure would." She followed him to his car and put her pack into the

Finding the Family of Killers

trunk that he opened for her. "Let me fill it up for you. That way you can just get inside and rest."

"Mighty nice of you. I will just let you do that." Zeke smiled as he headed back for the driver's seat. He could already feel his heartbeat increasing and his sense of pleasure increased along with it as he was already picturing Lori's end.

When Lori heard the pump click off, she closed the tank and put away the handle. She walked back inside and retrieved Zeke's change. It took scarcely a minute before she was inside the passenger seat with the door shut. "Here's your change." Lori handed it to Zeke.

"You keep it. Buy yourself some nice dinner." Zeke answered because he did not want anything that she had touched. He already had the car started and pulled out before asking Lori which way.

Lori didn't really care which way because she was on a holiday now that her boyfriend kicked her out. She sat silently and watched the turns this man took. She needed to know where she was when he let her out of the car if he let her out.

Zeke drove along a few miles before asking her where she wanted to go. If she picked the path, things would be easier for him. He was an old man now and she was young and strong. "Pick a direction because I need to get on with my own things." There, that would put it on her.

"Do you have time to drive up the pass an exit or two?" Lori had heard of some nice walks up to some lakes up there.

Bobbie Kaald

Zeke look at her and smiled. "That might be nice, but I will just drop you off and the next car can pick you up."

Two hours later, Zeke was heading home. He was whistling. Lori lay in a grave off the road with her pack and the car was wiped down and sweet smelling as if she had never been in his car. His heart never even skipped a beat until he had to dig his own hole. That was difficult but it was all filled in now and covered with last fall's leaves, needles, twigs, and cones from the rest of the forest floor. Every inch looked the same as places where he had never been.

Zeke was nearly back to the turn off for the junkyard, but he needed gas again. He would find a different station this time to avoid suspicion. This took a little longer than usual because he had to wait his turn. He used his time well by listening to the latest gossip. It seems a woman was killed, and her boy was missing.

Zeke topped off the tank and drove straight back to the yard. Someone had been busy, and they would need to leave right away. As he drove into the yard, a truck loaded with scrap was just turning out. 'Time to go, boys.' He felt anger and fear at the same time. He was not used to having other's lives interfere with his.

Finding the Family of Killers

If he hadn't gone off half cocked with the girl, he wouldn't be holding things up. No matter, he was ready to leave anyway. Tory was just walking away from the gate when Zeke drove up and Tory reopened it for Zeke. "Where have you been? How long does it take to get gas?"

"I had to get gas twice." Zeke answered back. "You ready to leave?"

"That we are. I picked up a young convert. He was glad to leave and even helped me with his mom. She had been beating him." Tory commented as they road up to the yard to pick up the others.

"No matter, they are looking for him in town. Probably looking for him everywhere." Zeke gave a short answer because he was trying to think of a way out of here. There would be roadblocks for certain.

Zeke swung the car around with gravel flying for an immediate exit when everyone was inside of the car. He hadn't turned the car off. Tory jumped out of the running car and went inside the falling apart office to roust everyone out for an immediate exit.

Zeke heard a lot of yelling and a minute later men started exiting the office. No one was really complaining, just making remarks. The youngest member, now a blonde, started to get into the front but saw Zeke pointing to the back and the boy did as suggested.

Bobbie Kaald

The older men climbed into the car after the boy, effectively blocking him in place. Zeke put the car into drive and didn't stop until he passed the gate. Stopping the car, Lane opened his door, but Tory was already out and nearly to the gate. Lane closed his door, grateful for Tory's allowing him to remain seated. It would have taken far longer to let Lane close the gate.

Tory returned to his place in the car and closed the door. "Pick your path Zeke. None of them are a good choice from what you said in the past."

"We will be guided by luck as is our usual. Perhaps a place not far from here if anyone remembers one, now is the time." Zeke headed north when he reached the road. South would be suicide as the town where he got gas twice was there.

Zeke drove on though the ever-increasing darkness down the heavily wooded section of a switchback road. It ran along the base of the foothills and was simply a paved over wagon road as were many of the roads in the Pacific Northwest. The trees were thick, and he was traveling without his lights on. This way even overhead surveillance wouldn't see them most of the time. Zeke liked these side roads for just that reason.

Anticipating roadblocks for the boy, Zeke planned to turn off and head cross country on a not so well traveled road. If they could make it to the turn off without a roadblock, they would be fine. Behind him, the two men and the boy sat silently. Each

Finding the Family of Killers

thinking their own thoughts. Hopefully planning how to handle a roadblock.

Zeke was nearly hypnotized by the road, but he still watched the road signs as he passed. When he could see up ahead, he counted cars. If there were too many, he would have to turn around somehow. U-turns on a two-lane road with oncoming traffic were nearly impossible. An absence of oncoming traffic signified an upcoming roadblock, and he would have to turn or turn around.

A short while later, Zeke decided to turn off the main road. With the relief that Zeke now felt, he opened conversation for everyone. "Tory, did you find a new name for your boy?" He assumed the boy was Tory's since Michael was Sam's and Sam was Tory's.

"I thought that he could choose a new name. Something he has never heard of before and this is not an easy task." Tory answered. "He asked for blonde hair because he was never allowed to dye his hair or bleach it before."

"I have been thinking about that." The boy spoke up with a high-pitched voice more than a little feminine. "I heard you and Lane talking. You all have new names for your new lives. Is that to make it difficult for you to be found?"

"That is most of it. Also, if we are caught, no one can reveal the other's real name." Zeke interjected because he is the one who started that name change business.

Bobbie Kaald

"I like that. I always liked the name, Phillip. It has a soft friendly sound to it." The boy with the blonde hair said and then looked to Tory for approval.

"Very nice, Phillip it is." Tory smiled at the young boy. They were always so eager to please at this young age.

Phillip was smiling now. He had a new name just like all the men. He was a man now, in his own mind. Mostly, Phillip was just trying to fit in and make the best of his new home. He couldn't go back because his mother was dead, and he didn't have a father. This would be his chosen foster home from now on.

Finding the Family of Killers

The Chase

Michael drove down to the Ghost Town every day, now. He was certain they would show up. He went to the junkyard and looked around. No one was there and he wasn't certain how long since the last time anyone had stayed here. There were signs of vehicles coming and going, but this was the rainy season, again. It rained too much here to know if the vehicles had been here within a week or a year.

When Michael stopped at the filling stations, no one could tell him if anyone different had been through. There were so many people coming and going that they had no idea. Certainly, there were no young boys without their parents.

Bobbie Kaald

Frustrated beyond belief, Michael arrived home at nearly midnight and parked on the street. He forgot how late it was and slammed his car door shut as he got out. The noise even made him jump. 'Oh, Oh, Roberts is going to be very unhappy.'

Michael tried to make negligible noise the rest of the way inside. The key turned silently in the lock, but the lock seemed to shout as it clicked open. Michael's skin jumped and nearly locked in place and his neck tightened up as well. Turning the doorknob, Michael slowly opened the door inward, but stopped because Roberts was yelling from the back of the house.

"Come in, Michael. The entire neighborhood has been calling to let me know how happy they are with your loud return." Roberts of course was being very sarcastic. He did that when he was trying to sleep.

Michael smiled and shut the door softly. Since, Roberts did not appear in person, Michael walked directly into his room and shut the door as he got ready for bed.

Michael was going into the office tomorrow to talk with James about the boy who had gone missing. It was many hours before he fell asleep and because of this, he was late getting up and going to work. Having missed breakfast, Michael stopped for two espressos on the way to the police station.

"Coffee, James." Michael asked with a cool air of innocence when he finally managed to grace the doorframe of the police station.

Finding the Family of Killers

"Where have you been for the last week? I wish you were still on probation, then I would know where you were." James put his hand over the phone receiver as he yelled this at Michael.

Michael put James coffee on his desk and took his over to the spare chair where he sat down abruptly. "If you must know, I have been looking for the missing boy. I have been at the Ghosts Town all day, every day, for the last week. No one knows anything. No one remembers the men or the boy or strangers either. I am very frustrated."

"Thanks for the coffee." James answered when Michael took a break in his diatribe. "I have not heard anything either. I know you're upset about the boy's abduction, but we will find him."

"You will try, but you were always a step behind. That's why I have been looking. I know some places where they might go to rest and begin indoctrinating the boy." Michael admitted something he had never said aloud before. "Wolfe knows some as well, but he is afraid of me because he is afraid of the men."

"Really. Okay, where have you been for a week?" James was all ears now as he began to see Michael in a whole new light.

"You remember that Ghost Town down south. The one that the two women disappeared into." Michael answered James immediately mostly because he needed help. He already told him, but he was willing to repeat it.

Bobbie Kaald

"Yes, the very one you were just babbling about." James was trying not to laugh, but sometimes Michael just could not get to the point.

"So, I did." Michael took the last drink of his now cold coffee and just sat there supposedly thinking.

"You found nothing in a week except a bunch of people who told you that they knew absolutely nothing." James began summarizing Michael's plight.

"That is exactly what I didn't find." Michael sat holding his head in his hands. He nearly cried but he had not cried since his own abduction many years ago until this case.

James saw how upset Michael was and chose to let the conversation drop for now. If Michael was beginning to open up, he didn't want to be the one to shut the door.

As the two men sat doing their own thing, someone entered the station and let the door shut loudly as it always did when allowed to do so on its own accord.

"James, is Michael in there?" If was Wolfe's voice and not Roberts as they expected. He walked into the office as if he had never driven out of town as if forever.

"Wolfe! Where have you been?" Michael jumped up and nearly hugged Wolfe, but his past would not allow this action.

"Around. Michael, I came back because I now realize what you were talking about. If you were around that for years, I just

Finding the Family of Killers

am amazed as to how well you turned out." Wolfe was blabbering on and on until finally Michael interrupted.

"Okay, I get it, Wolfe." Michael smiled because he thought that Wolfe was intending on staying here. "I'm glad that your back. Roberts and I drove after you but only found Tory and then lost him."

"You're kidding. You two did that?" Wolfe was shocked at this after nearly running Michael over the night he left town.

"Alright, we are all glad that you're back. Have you been home, yet?" James interrupted loudly because he needed to bust up the reminiscence meeting on work time. Always the rain cloud without a silver lining.

Wolfe was silent for a mini second before answering, "No. I'm going now." He turned and left immediately. James was right about needing to go home and talk to his parents. He had been angry when he left and that was no way to leave things.

Michael turned to James and the two of them resumed their conversation. "You know what I think. It was easier to figure out the next step when Roberts had his men here."

James looked startled, "I guess it was. We do have that large room in the basement. If you want to organize it, maybe we can get Roberts to volunteer his time. He's so busy being retired and all." James put up a hand to stop Michael from asking the obvious question. "Before you ask, I have no idea what kind of equipment is down there. Everything from the old shop on first street went straight down there."

Bobbie Kaald

"Can I have a key to keep?" Michael knew he was pushing it, but he felt the need to ask."

"If I have at least two keys for the door, I think that would be a good idea. If not, you can take the key and verify that it works before going and making three copies. That way we have the original in the key cupboard, and each of us will have one." James stood up and moved one step toward the wall where the keys were. When he opened the box, he could only smile. There were five keys. "Okay, take all these keys to the downstairs door and verify that they open it. Come back with all of them and we can disperse the keys."

Michael smiled and took the keys. He turned and left the office. He was back in less than five minutes with the keys. "They all work." Handing them all back to James and he remained standing in front of the desk.

James looked up at Michael. "You are too fast. I just can't get any work done." He gave Michael one key and put two on his ring. Getting up, he turned and put the last two back on the hook where he took them from and closed the box. "Roberts is meeting us at his favorite restaurant for lunch. Come and be my buddy to get him to volunteer his expertise."

"You know me, I can always eat." Michael turned and began walking toward the door leading out of the office. He stopped when he saw the weather outside. It was now a deluge of rain

Finding the Family of Killers

so hard that it splashed off the ground when the drops hit. "I will come outside when you get my door unlocked."

"It's just across the street. Where were you born anyway?" James laughed as he let himself out.

Michael was frowning as he let himself out. Walking had its drawbacks when you forgot your coat at home.

Bobbie Kaald

The Bakery

Isaac spent many days cleaning and weeks setting up his new place. He only had enough money for a token size business when he opened. Before that happened, he wanted to take a vacation to get his stress level down.

When Isaac started preparing for his vacation, he put new newspaper over the windows. He obtained a roll from the local newspaper printing office and rolled it out on the floor and cut it to fit. When this was done, he tacked it around the edges with great difficulty. He could barely climb the ladder. His knees were beginning to lock, and the pain was severe as he tried to bend them for the next rung.

Finding the Family of Killers

After hours of pain, Isaac collapsed onto the floor at the bottom of the ladder. He slowly lay the rest of the way down and tried to calm himself. His breathing was short and shallow. He needed a deep breath, but he could not take enough air in. His heart was beating too fast. He closed his eyes and forced himself to slow his breathing. After what seemed to be forever, Isaac managed a deep breath, and he couldn't feel his heartbeat quite so much. He lay there for another minute or two before sitting up.

"Food and bed for me. The ladder will be here when I get back." Isaac muttered to himself as he rolled to his side and muttered under his breath about how he ever got such a fool idea to do this all on his own. He needed more help.

Isaac stood up and went to the back door. He checked to see if it was locked, and it was. On the way back to the front door, Isaac stopped by the phone. He made two calls, one to turn off the water and one to turn off the electricity. He then called to turn off the phone. With that done, Isaac was ready for his trip.

Smiling like a teenage boy going to the prom, Isaac walked outside and turned to close and lock the door. He hadn't closed the door in days while he was working because he liked to listen to the conversation pieces as people walked by.

Isaac's car was always packed with sleeping bags and his shave kit in the trunk. That's all he really needed except the shovel that he kept in the trunk as well. He told people it was so he could bury his garbage, keep the environment clean, and

Bobbie Kaald

put out the fire he might start to cook dinner. Laughing to himself, Isaac climbed in and started his car up. He would eat later.

With the car started and running smooth, Isaac backed out slowly and headed south. A quick drive-by of his bakery couldn't hurt. He wouldn't get out. He just wanted to see if it was still standing after all the volcanic activity. He really wanted to stay here because there was only a small amount ash this far north. Even with the north side falling off, the ash went up so high that the jet stream took it east by south-east and then south-west.

Isaac would go south to the freeway and west to the valley road. From there, it would depend on any bridges being closed. At any rate, Isaac would get a nice drive. He always felt relaxed after a long drive.

Still smiling, Isaac drove past the last small town before the mountain pass. He should have left earlier in the day because it was already getting dark. His planning and thoughts started to consider the junkyard. He hadn't been there for years. Bill and the others had already left it when Isaac ran into the family by his bakery.

It was completely dark before Isaac reached the first town on the west side. Glancing down at the fuel gauge, he saw that he was nearly out of gas. Coasting would help to conserve what little gas there was in the tank, but not much.

Finding the Family of Killers

Isaac breathed a sigh of relief when he reached the first gas station on his road. Junk food travel dinner coming up.

Isaac automatically went to the family's usual gas station and pulled in. He parked by the pump and got out. Going inside, he grabbed a few items and a paper. "I'll get this and thirty on pump three." As he walked out, two men were talking about a boy who was missing. They were looking at a poster.

Isaac put his purchases into the car and began running the gas into his tank. He couldn't hear what the men were saying. When the pump clicked off, Isaac put the hose away and closed up his tank. Full of curiosity, he walked over and looked at the poster. Clearly, Tory was busy again. The boy's mother was found dead in their house, but the boy was missing.

On impulse, Isaac went inside to pick-up a few more things to eat in case he spent the night on the side of the road, so to speak. By the time Issac bought his food and left the mini grocery, he also learned that a man had been in here every day for a couple of weeks looking for certain men and a boy. This was interesting to Isaac. He felt that the man was undoubtedly Michael who had also been abducted after his mother was killed by Tory's protégé.

Isaac walked out with his purchases and climbed inside of his car. He was feeling left out and uninformed. As he drove south toward his former bakery, Isaac began formulating a new plan. He was now firm in his decision to just do a drive by look see at the former bakery. His interest was growing in the activities of

Bobbie Kaald

his family of men. He knew he should stay on a separate path, but he was curious as to how many were still on the move and how many may have been arrested. He also thought it might be nice to meet this new boy.

Finding the Family of Killers

Phillip

Phillip woke up the next morning in a different bed. He began to think this might be his new norm. The men seemed to move a lot and Phillip was okay with this. Also, as an added bonus, there was no discussion of his going to school. Not to mention that he didn't have to worry about his mother beating him for just being a child and accidentally breaking something. He felt relief for the first time in his life.

"Phillip, come and eat before they forget to leave you some." Tory's voice came in from the other room. He had his own room here, another first for him.

"Coming." Phillip called back as he jumped up and put his shoes on first thing. The house was less than clean, and Tory

Bobbie Kaald

had told him about finding a lot of used syringes at one house that he stopped at. He also told him in vivid detail what kind of diseases lay invisibly on the used syringes. Dying would be the best thing those diseases could do and did for people.

"I'm here." Phillip went over to the place where Tory told him to eat while they were here to wait. He knew what his mom would do if he didn't mind to the letter. He didn't want to know what a man capable of murder without a thought would do to him if he didn't follow the new rules.

"Alright, here's your breakfast. Put the plate in the fire when you're done and then we leave." Tory brought him a paper plate of buttered pancakes and turned around to clean up the rest of the house. "We need to leave this as if we had never been here. The fire will cool and then all evidence will be gone."

Zeke and Lane listened as they cleaned up their own mess. Their plates were in the fire already. "We can get gasoline on the way." Zeke mentioned on his way out to the car with Lane close behind them.

Phillip was full after two pancakes but choked down the third. He drank enough water to wash down the feeling of choking and took the glass to the sink. Throwing the rest of the water down the sink, Phillip took his glass and plate to the fire. It was really hot, but he managed to throw the plate and glass into the fire. It flamed up quickly and soon was fully engulfed. He would have watched until the end, but he was expected in the car.

Finding the Family of Killers

Tory watched Phillip's fascination with fire. He knew that it was common for a young man to like fire, but not a good thing if he started salivating when he watched. Phillip walked out the door in front of Tory who closed the door behind himself. He would watch Phillip before he decided that Phillip was a keeper. Arsonists weren't allowed in the group and not one of the others would make the call, but they were waiting for Tory to make the call.

"Get a move on will ya?" Lane called out from the car. "We've a long way to go today." Lane really had no plans, but he loved to harass the others. He especially liked to watch Phillip jump. He would do his part to bring Phillip into the fold.

Bobbie Kaald

Reunion

Isaac drove through the night and managed to find his bakery. He parked in front of it and sat for a few minutes absorbing the comfort of the air around him. He missed this place and all the people who treated him like a friend or a family member. Treated him like he was normal when in his heart he knew he was not.

Getting out, Isaac put his first foot down and puffs of dirt swirled around from the small air currents of his movement. Could this be that ash still around? Two plus years later? Isaac had no doubts about that and confirmed it by slamming the door shut and watching the fluff swirl up to his knees.

Finding the Family of Killers

Isaac thought about his trip down here as he walked up to the front door. The one-way bridges and debris everywhere along the way. The closer he got, the more debris there was.

When Isaac got to the door, he tried unlocking the door just for kicks. It opened and he went inside. Looking around there was ash everywhere having egressed through every possible crevice. Minimal cobwebs from only the highest possible areas, but no spiders could be seen. They must not like the ash. Isaac didn't either. He turned around and walked back out, closing, and locking the door behind him again.

Breakfast was calling Isaac who hadn't eaten in too long to remember. He walked his usual path as if he did so every day and had never left. The diner looked to be open and functioning as it had in the past. The same old cars seemed to be here just as if the mountain never turned back into a volcano.

Entering the diner, Isaac was all smiles. His favorite waitress was working today. "Maggie! How are you doing? Menu the same?"

"Isaac! We thought that you were dead. You disappeared and the volcano blew, and you never came back." Maggie ran over to give Isaac a hug but stopped as he backed away. "Still not a hugger?"

"You know that. Let me sit at the big table okay?" Isaac was feeling nostalgic. He didn't expect company but wanted to have lots of leg room.

Bobbie Kaald

"Business is still slow so you should be okay to sit at the table for six by yourself." Maggie spoke without a sarcastic tone to her voice as she turned and went to fetch the coffee pot. She knew that Isaac was weird and didn't question him wanting the table for six. It was in the corner and made him feel secure, she guessed. When she turned back around, Isaac was already sliding into place. He lifted his cup and turned it upside down to show that it was empty. "Still the same Isaac." She laughed at his antics because it reminded her of before the volcano. It had been so dead around here since then, no pun intended.

"I see my place is still empty. What gives?" Isaac asked as nonchalantly as he could.

"After the eruption, a lot of the businesses just closed. I think the whole building is owned by the bank now." Maggie smiled and pulled out her pad. "The usual breakfast? Omelet?"

"I think a ham and cheese omelet would go down just fine." Isaac watched her walk away and then picked up his coffee. He quickly became lost in thought while he waited, as per his usual thought processes when he was sitting alone.

"Isaac are you back here?" Tory asked and then laughed when Isaac jumped perceptibly.

"Just for the day. I am on a drive to rest. I have just spent many months fixing up my new place in Eastern Washington." Isaac answered and waived them into the booth.

Finding the Family of Killers

In a near whisper, Tory asked after Isaac's identity change. "Your name?" He watched and Isaac nodded, and Tory nodded back. "This young man is my sister's boy, Phillip, and with me are Lane and Zeke."

"Lane and Zeke, I remember. I'm Isaac. As I was saying, my old bakery is vacant. I hear the whole building is owned by the bank now." Isaac smiled at the young man with Tory. He looked to be a good choice but only time would tell.

Just then Maggie arrive carrying Isaac's food. "Friends of yours? I bet some pancakes are on the order." After putting down Isaac's food, she pulled her pad out and waited for their order.

Tory smiled at her and noted her name tag. "Maggie, you are correct, I believe. Phillip, two pancakes and a side of bacon?"

"Orange juice too?" Phillip was happy now. He didn't usually have time to finish eating with the family's time schedule.

"That's a wise choice." Tory looked at Maggie and continued with his order. "What Isaac is having and coffee and orange juice for Phillip."

Lane looked at Isaac devouring his food. "Make that two of Isaac's order. Cream would be nice with my coffee."

Zeke wanted what the others ordered but decided on, "Two pancakes, two eggs sunny side up, and a side of bacon with my coffee."

Bobbie Kaald

"Got it. It will be just a minute. Seconds, Isaac?" Maggie asked as he put a bite into his mouth. She laughed and walked away.

"I nearly choked, no thanks Maggie." Isaac called after her when he felt able to speak. "She does like her little jokes."

Phillip's eyes were on Isaac's toast that went uneaten. He couldn't ask but he could look.

"You want my toast. I can't stuff it down." Isaac held out the toast on a small plate to Phillip.

Tory handed it to Phillip. "Thank-you. I am hungry." Phillip loved buttered toast and ate it quickly as if it might disappear.

"I stopped to get gas at a mini grocery north of here. Seems they had a visitor often enough to get noticed. A former friend of yours, Tory." Isaac casually mentioned this information full of shock value without a name.

"Sorry that I missed him. Maybe next time we might meet." Tory took a drink of his coffee which is what he really wanted as a way to wake up. He kept his eyes mostly closed in case knives were shooting out of them because of the news.

"I need to get back to my store. Maybe you want to bring Phillip with you and come to see what the potential is." Isaac stated as a way of suggesting splitting the team. "If Lane and Zeke want to stay here, I have a key to the bakery. You could check with the bank about living there or re-opening it."

Finding the Family of Killers

"Not much of a baker, and at my age, running a business isn't in the cards for me." Lane put his two cents in.

Conversation stopped as their food came. Maggie handed it out without asking which was who's order. After she left, Zeke added. "I like to bake, but it wouldn't be out at the crack of dawn like most bakeries."

"Not much of a morning person?" Isaac asked to keep the conversation flowing.

"Not really. Isn't there another bakery around here?" Zeke asked because he had heard of a specialty bakery.

"So, I found out when we left a couple of years ago." Isaac's voice was filled with sarcasm as he said this.

"I could do specialty items. Cupcakes, cakes, donuts." Zeke said between bites.

By the time the group finished eating, it was decided. Tory and Isaac would head to Isaac's new store with Phillip. Phillip remained silent due to his building fear of these men. He listened intently and tried to find out anything he could. However, the men revealed nothing from his perspective. He didn't understand the talk was in a code of sorts.

Zeke and Lane remained in town. Now in possession of the key, they decided to sleep in the car due to the ash inside the store that Isaac informed them of. They would make an offer

Bobbie Kaald

on the building with the money from the scrap metal run. They gave Tory a small amount and he would get more money later.

Isaac left copious funds on the table as they left and went their way. He gave a wave to Maggie to let her know the family was leaving.

Finding the Family of Killers

Natasha and Helena

Neither girl wanted to talk about what they learned at dinner when they stopped in uninvited at Natasha's parent's house. Helena arrived late the next morning to find the shop still locked. Thinking the worst, she called Natasha on her new cell phone. There was no answer. Helena decided to go around back.

When she turned the corner into the alley, Helena began to shake more than a little. Never-the-less, she continued. Always looking in every direction, Helena walked until she could view the back door. Natasha wasn't there either.

Helena sighed and pulled out her key to the back door. Just as she was about to insert it, she remembered setting the New

Bobbie Kaald

York apartment bar lock before leaving last night. She put away the key and walked back the way she had come.

When she turned the last corner, Helena saw that the front door was already open. "Sorry that I'm late, Natasha called out to her."

"I forgot that I can't get in the back with the key." Helena admitted and then continued. "I want to talk about the night at your mom's." She just blurted it out so that she couldn't chicken out.

Natasha looked up at her but didn't answer. She continued opening the store. "After work." That is all that Natasha said and then turned her back to continue her work. Her brain was going a thousand miles per hour. She thought Helena didn't want to discuss it. Natasha thought that she would call her mom when Helena went to lunch.

Helena paled and nearly collapsed. Natasha never told her no, but then she didn't really say no, she only said after work. Helena muttered many things under her breath as she walked into the back room to begin her part of the job.

Finding the Family of Killers

The Search

Michael worked at the speed of light when he wanted to. This was one of those times. It only took him about an hour to clean everything, and another half of an hour to sweep the dirt off the floor. He would have to clean again tomorrow when the dust settled. He could never remember to do the floor first and then dust.

After that he stood back and looked at what was present as far as equipment and furniture and tried to decide where things should go. After that, he just started moving things over by the walls and whatever was left went into the center of the room.

The desks were left and knowing that everyone would have an opinion as to where they should go. He put them all touching

Bobbie Kaald

each other in the center of the room to allow discussion as well as independent investigations. It was kind of like a big meeting table but with desk space for four.

When he was done, Michael collapsed into a chair. He had exhausted all of his energy reserve. He was smiling because he liked what he saw, and he had done it all on his own without coaching. 'It must be getting late', he thought to himself.

Just then a voice came down the stairs, "Michael are you ready for the big reveal or do you need any help." It was Roberts voice and he sounded sincere.

"I needed help an hour ago but come on down and see if you have anything to add." Michael was laughing and too tired to get up.

Heavy footsteps came down the stairs, men's boot probably. "First time I ever saw this room clean." Roberts made his first observation.

"You've been down here?" Michael was astounded.

"Yes and no. When I first arrived, I was going to come down here, but James showed me a picture and that was enough to let me know it was too small." Roberts didn't go into detail. He didn't even remember the exact total number of dead person's remains that they discovered back then, and he didn't want to remind Michael.

Finding the Family of Killers

"Come all the way in and see if you can work with this." Michael encouraged Roberts to come in and stood up to walk beside Roberts as he spoke.

"Nicely arranged, and I like the central desks because we can see each other when we talk, and still work." Roberts talked as they walked. "Tomorrow we can go to the office supply store and load up with things we will need."

"Good. Right now, I am off to find food." Michael turned and headed for the stairs, abandoning Roberts. He could hear Roberts laughing as he came along behind him.

"How does it look, Roberts?" James had his hand on the front door handle preparing to leave for the day. He turned back to speak to them as he heard them making for his office.

"Very usable. Michael and I are heading for dinner. You heading home, are you? I guess you will have to wait until tomorrow for a look." Roberts called after James who was already outside.

James mumbled something and then turned around. "Have a look at the fax on my desk before you leave." With that, James got in his cruiser and started his drive home. He hated to ruin their night, but they needed to know.

"What is that all about?" Michael asked as he turned and went over to James desk. His door was open and should be closed as James custom on leaving for the day. He reached for the fax, but Roberts snatched it away. Turning he looked over Roberts shoulder.

Bobbie Kaald

"It would appear that another woman has disappeared. Let's just leave it here for tomorrow when we will take everything downstairs and start the hunt." Roberts put the fax down where James left it and turned to leave. "Let's get something to take home with us. We can get an early night that way and be back here for an early start in the morning."

"That is a great idea." Michael followed Roberts out to his car. "Maybe we can try that new hand-out."

"I like that idea. It's a bit out of the way, but it should be worth it in the long run." Roberts climbed in and unlocked Michael's door. When they were both in, he started the car and headed out of town. He had heard the food there was excellent, but he would miss the other hand-out's food that he had his heart set on.

The drive took them north out of town and past the fruit stand that was closed until next season. Roberts was still unused to the back roads and drove the way he knew. Pulling into the hand-out, he saw there was a line, but they were serving from both sides. "This should go quickly. Do you know what you want?"

"Two of whatever you're having. Here's some money. James gave me an advance because you are spending too much money on feeding me." Michael handed Roberts a couple of twenties. "My treat tonight."

Finding the Family of Killers

The Bakery

Lane spent his days trying to get an occupancy permit for the bakery and the living quarters. He was not in love with the procedure because there was always something else to fix. It irritated him to feel agitated with the system. After all, it was just the system, not the employee's fault. Still, it annoyed him not to be able to move in and begin setting up right away.

Zeke spent his time looking around the rest of the town and drove up to where the road was blocked off. When he returned, he talked to Lane. "I think there is too much limelight here. Everyone knows our faces now. This is not a good thing. It is making me feel too uncomfortable."

Bobbie Kaald

"You feel that, too? I found myself stalking a single woman today." Lane admitted to Zeke and sighed. "We are very well known now because Isaac lived here for a long time and those people still here have all introduced themselves to us. I'm ready to leave because we may never get permission to open the bakery."

"I'm glad that you talked to them. I hate inspectors and all their questions." Zeke responded. "Okay then, let's leave in the morning."

"I think that's best." Lane said as he got up and walked over to where his blankets were.

Lane and Zeke left the bakery before the sun came up. They drove north discussing their options. Both men were glad that Phillip was not with them. They wouldn't have to feel the least amount of guilt if there were still roadblocks.

There weren't any roadblocks on the route that they drove. It was just one of many backroads through the county. The grass grew right up to the blacktop even though the county sprayed poison every summer. The trees grew tall enough for the branches to nearly reach each other over the road.

"Wasn't there a road where the branches touched the ones on the other side of the road, and it was like a tunnel driving

Finding the Family of Killers

through it?" Zeke asked Lane. He was feeling nostalgic. He did his first on that street.

"I always loved that street. We went fishing there on many different occasions." Lane had different memories of the street Zeke referred to. "That street is miles north of here."

"Why don't we look for some place up there?" Zeke was trying to be helpful but actually needed to go there. His internal drive had awakened.

"You think it is still out in the woods, so to speak?" Lane said aloud for both of their hearing. Zeke didn't answer because Lane continued. "We might as well look. It would be a good place if it is still isolated."

They drove on in silence. Noon came and went, and the two men remained silent and lost in their own thoughts. "Coffee?" Lane asked out of the blue.

"Always. Listening to the gossip is a good thing also." Zeke didn't want to break the mood, but he had a headache the size of Vesuvius from his body crying out for caffeine.

"McDonalds then. Food is average, but people talk a lot there." Lake answered Zeke in passing because the traffic was picking up as they neared the next town.

Bobbie Kaald

Open

Tory did most of the driving after the dinner with Lane and Zeke. He decided to drive the way they fled the mountain and see it in some type of lighting. It was nice to be able to see the edge of the road now that the ash was mostly settled. "Are you doing okay, Phillip?" He didn't want any accidents because Phillip was afraid to speak his needs.

"I don't know about Phillip, but I need to take a leak in a major way." Isaac spoke from the passenger seat. They let the boy have the back and be able to stretch out if he got tired.

Finding the Family of Killers

"Is there anything to eat or drink after we take a leak as Isaac said?" Phillip was leaning up against the center of the front seat as he spoke.

"What is rule number one when riding in a car?" Tory asked without answering either of the two with him.

"Buckle up." Phillip answered as he slid back and clipped his belt into place.

"I believe we can take care of all of the issues just up ahead a couple of miles." Tory said and smiled. He was pretty certain that Isaac needed to go before that after all the coffee that he drank at the diner.

"I need you to pull over right away." Isaac finally admitted his reality and turned to look straight at Tory. He was thinking of the things he would do to Tory if he didn't stop. Tory might be younger, but Isaac knew some tricks.

"Right you are." Tory braked hard and swerved all over the road before sliding to a stop on the right-hand side. "Immediate results as you require. Phillip, please get out on Isaac's side and leave the door open. It will block what you are doing in case someone comes. Isaac, you go first and when you're done, I will go."

With the impromptu latrine business complete, the men and the boy climbed back inside. Tory drove on the same way they were heading. "Next stop, dinner."

Phillip was buckled in and smiling. He was getting very hungry now that his bladder was empty. More room for his

Bobbie Kaald

empty stomach to feel empty he guessed. Also, he always got very hungry after someone brought up food. He was wondering what kind of business Isaac started at this new place they were going to. Maybe he would ask when they stopped to eat.

Isaac took over driving after their dinner stop. Tory reclined against the window of the passenger seat and was instantly asleep. Phillip lay in the backseat, belted in but moaning. He ate every bite and was now extremely sorry.

Isaac took the scenic route because he had no choice. The road Tory started on had no turnoffs. It took hours before they found another city. Tory sat up about then and looked around.

"I think this is where we first came out of the ash." Tory commented just because he was thinking about it.

"Just like back then, we need to gas up." Isaac said as he pulled into the station. With the engine off, the three family members got out. "Phillip, make good use of the stop and start with the men's room."

Tory and Phillip walked inside and left Isaac to fill up the car. When Isaac was done, he walked slowly into the station with his ears open for any and all information, good or bad for them.

No new news was a good thing, and they were soon on their way to parts known only to Isaac. Isaac prepared himself with

Finding the Family of Killers

caffeine to keep himself awake and a Three Musketeers bar for later.

"You never said what kind of business you intend to run." Tory felt like talking and didn't really care what kind of business because it meant nothing to him.

"I hadn't really decided, but I guess an odds and end shop mixed with a hardware store. What do you think?" Isaac didn't look at Tory because he was driving.

"As good as any. You don't really intend to run a store, do you?" Tory's voice was full of sarcasm and disgust.

"It helps me meet new people. That's why I ran the bakery and still fulfilled my urges." Isaac laughed then. Why they tried to justify what they did, he would never know.

Tory dosed off and Isaac continued to drive toward his newest illusion of reality. He liked to arrive after dark especially with the newest additions to his staff. Phillip would need to be kept low profile and there-by bypass most visual checks of the school employees. Tory had already mocked together a school history from out of state just in case someone found Phillip. He always cited religious preferences for the reason they home schooled.

Isaac administered a placement test to Phillip as a way of verifying what his education was and it did correspond to his age of ten years. As he drove into town, he stopped letting his mind wander and focused on finding the alley behind his

Bobbie Kaald

business. Pulling into his buildings parking spot, Isaac turned off the car. "Everyone out, we have arrived."

Isaac got out and walked up to the rear entrance of his place. Unlocking the door, he opened it and then returned to the car. He never took very much with him, but what he needed to go inside of his place. His sleeping bag would double as his blanket on the mattress and tomorrow, he would have to find two more mattresses.

When they were all inside, Tory looked around. "Not ready to open yet?"

"Almost, but I wanted to take a trip first. We will have to sleep in shifts until we get more mattresses." Isaac was not prepared for a larger family.

"That's alright. We're used to making do." Tory put his arm around Phillip. "Let's find a place to sleep."

Finding the Family of Killers

Growing Family

Zeke and Lane stayed in a nineteen twenty type flea bag motel somewhere in Eastern Washington for several days. They ate at local restaurants and walked through town for hours on end, getting exercise.

After a week of this, Lane went out one night alone. When he came back, he woke Zeke up. "We are leaving. I am bored and active, again."

"Right, I'm up. Get your stuff while I dress and pee." Zeke mumbled on his way to the bathroom. He was already active again and only wondered when Lane would get the urge. He met Lane in the car just a few minutes later. "Where to?"

Bobbie Kaald

"Around, I just don't feel the love here." Lane put the car into reverse and backed out of the parking spot before putting it into drive and heading for parts unknown.

Lane leaned back and was asleep before Zeke drove out of the parking lot. Being up all night tends to do that to a person. He dreamed of his activities last night and his heartbeat quickened so that his chest caused him enough pain to wake him up. "Can we find a bed soon? I believe that I need a few days of rest."

Zeke looked over at Lane and saw he was pale and sweating. This was not a good thing. Certainly, Isaac could let them stay with him. He wished that he remembered what Isaac had said about where his new place was. "First motel for some rest. I'll search for Isaac while you sleep. I can bring back food every night."

Lane didn't answer. He was awake but his eyes were closed. Only he knew that he was trying every relaxation technique that he ever heard of. "Maybe a bottle of aspirin. I hear that helps prevent extending heart attacks and strokes. It can't hurt." He said this all one word at a time. He was in a bad way and he was certain that Zeke knew it, now.

Finding the Family of Killers

Murder Board

Michael awakened early because he was anxious to get started on the files and placing the files up around the room by date. He wanted to be able to get a good look at the sequence of disappearances. He learned yesterday that his key for the basement room also fit into the back door. This gave him access to the station when the police were out on night patrol.

Michael should have checked the front door for any on duty police officers present before sneaking in the back way. When he let himself into the basement, he locked the back door behind himself and tried to start his plan for the day. At this all-important juncture, he realized that his personal files were still upstairs.

Bobbie Kaald

Michael sighed and walked upstairs hoping the door wasn't locked from this side. He did have a key, but he was already low on energy and decided that he should have eaten breakfast first, and coffee of course. The door opened to let him into the station proper and when he swung it open, he came face to face with the night officer who had his gun pointed at him.

"Michael? Are you sleeping here now?" the officer asked as he put the gun away. "I almost shot you. I hope you know that my chest hurts like a heart attack."

"Sorry. No, I am not sleeping here, but I woke up early and decided to get started. James gave me a key to the basement, and I found out that it opens the back door as well. I should have checked to see if you were in before entering, sorry again." Michael stumbled backward and just rattled off a long apology.

"Have some coffee with me and then get started. I need to calm down after that." The officer walked out to the desk in the front of the station and sat down by the phone. He picked up his coffee mug as if nothing had happened and began to drink the still steaming coffee.

Michael got himself a cup of coffee since the officer still had half a pot left. Walking over to the chair next to this man he had yet to meet, he sat down and took a sip of the black coffee. Michael made a face even though he tried not to. "How old is that coffee?"

Finding the Family of Killers

"Made it fresh when I got here, oh, about seven hours ago. You like it? I'm Roger, by the way. I don't think we have met, but I know of you. You are Michael and live with Roberts." Roger relaxed back in his chair and smiled all the time he was talking to Michael. He had red hair and a very relaxed attitude.

"You have me, Roger. Roberts is going to help me set up an investigation room in the basement. Feel free to bring copies of fliers down and look at the ones we will be posting." Michael got up and went back over to the coffee area and added copious dry creamer and sugar to the coffee. He was going to have a really acid stomach if he didn't. "I'm glad to meet you, but I wanted to get an early start. That is of course why I came in through the basement."

"Have at it. I will be off in an hour and stop down to see what you've done." Roger smiled and motioned for Michael to get on with his day.

Michael turned and walked over to his upstairs desk. He grabbed his files with his free hand. He continued to drink his doctored coffee as he walked back toward the basement door to get started with his tentative plan. He knew they would revise it as needed.

Bobbie Kaald

The End?

Lane woke up in the dark. He sat on the edge of the bed and looked around. He couldn't see a thing. Standing up slowly, he kept his right leg up against the mattress. This worked for the first two steps, but his kneecap impacted with the phone table between the beds. Swearing in four languages all of them unintelligible, he turned around and put his left leg against the mattress.

Lane walked more quickly now because he needed to find the bathroom soon. Walking around the bed, Lane crashed into something but managed to stay on his feet. After two more collisions, he reached the bathroom and found the light switch

Finding the Family of Killers

which he used. "Great, now I can see all of the germs." He spoke aloud and walked over to the toilet whose seat was down, but he left it. After urinating a large quantity, he flushed with toilet paper and washed without using the bar of used soap because it was cleaner. He returned to the bed without turning off the light because he didn't want any more accidents.

When Lane sat down, he noticed the other bed was still made and had a take-out brown bag on it that seemed to have grease spots on it. It was then that he realized his chest didn't hurt anymore and he wasn't as wobbly on his little adventure in the dark.

"Guess I bypassed the big one." Lane said aloud to himself and grabbed the bag to see what Zeke left for him. He ate quickly which brought back the chest pain. Throwing away the last of the food, he lay down and waited for it to pass.

Awakening a little while later, Lane opened his eyes to light coming around the edges of the black out curtains. "Morning at last."

"Yes, it is, and I am sleeping. There's money on the dresser for another day's food supply. We will leave after dark." Zeke said from the other bed.

"I will take care of that, thanks. I'm better. I think it is just my stomach. By the way, did you find Isaac?" Lane asked but got no answer. He stopped talking and got up to start his day while Zeke slept.

Bobbie Kaald

Later that day, well after dark as Zeke had said, the two men cleaned up the room and wiped down all the surfaces as was their habit before leaving. When they were satisfied, they left the key on the desk and walked out together. Lane shut the door quietly and joined Zeke in the car. Zeke would be driving because he knew the way.

Lane sat up and watched the turns that Zeke made. It was a mental game he played in his mind. He tried to guess where they would end up before it was obvious. It didn't work this time.

Zeke turned left off the main highway and drove down into the smallest town that Lane ever saw. The roads were paved, and the stores were brick or plaster. Every building needed a facelift and or new paint. Anymore run down and the buildings would simply collapse in on themselves.

Lane thought that surely this was a bypass, and they would go on. Next turn was a right into an alley and then he parked next to Isaac's old beater.

They got out and softly closed their doors. Zeke was about to knock when the door opened quietly, and Phillip stood there. He stepped back and allowed the two men to enter. Phillip closed the door behind them and locked it. After that, Phillip went upstairs to his bed because he was nearly asleep on his feet.

Finding the Family of Killers

Lane followed Phillip upstairs with Zeke right behind him. Neither were tired, but they lay down for some sleep because they could never predict what tomorrow would hold.

Bobbie Kaald

The Chase

Roberts arrived at about ten o'clock. It was his usual time to come to the station. He wanted James to arrive and take care of his morning phone call with the mayor before he arrived for a mug of coffee.

This morning Michael wasn't home for breakfast and he took his own sweet time soaking in the alone time that this allowed him. His serenity was all the way into his blood by the time he walked over to the police station.

When he opened the door, his serenity left. Everything was wild inside of the station and extra people materialized out of the very air since yesterday. "Hey, what's going on?"

Finding the Family of Killers

Five people ignored him totally, and a new man on the desk hung up the phone just then and addressed him. "Sir, can I help you?"

"Roberts, come here, quick." James yelled out of his office.

"James, you're the only person that I recognize." Roberts strode in a straight line directly into James' office. He totally ignored the new guy which was the wrong thing to do. A hand on his shoulder stopped him six inches from the door frame.

"Sir, you can't just walk in." The desk officer spoke softly for Roberts only.

"I was expecting him. We will be going into the basement for a morning briefing if anyone calls, Jerry." James got up and walked over to Roberts. His eyes never left Jerry's hand who slowly lifted his hand off Roberts' shoulder.

"Certainly, sir." Jerry turned and resumed his place behind the desk.

"Michael's waiting for us in the basement." James took the lead and walked the ten feet to the basement stairs.

"Who are all of these people?" Roberts asked as he looked around at the ten or so new people running around in brand new uniforms. He could tell the uniforms were new from the starched crease in the pants.

"Trainees the mayor sent me the class from the college for a week. I got a fourth of the class each week for the month. Lucky me." James opened the door in the middle of his answer and quickly disappeared down the stairs.

Bobbie Kaald

Roberts grabbed the door and entered slowly as the door closed behind him. He looked around and saw that Michael had assembled the files with sticky notes for things they knew or didn't know. "You pulled in early today."

"I couldn't sleep. I did meet Roger for coffee this morning." Michael answered as his way of saying how early he came in.

"I can clearly see that you got in early. Well organized in the way we used to have the offices. Have you any opinions, yet?" Roberts was walking around the room looking at the exhibits Michael put up for them. This was going to be just as daunting of a task as the one's before were.

"There are huge age differences here. When we did this before, they were mostly young. I think there must be more than one man involved at this point." Michael watched Roberts and James every move and where they stopped to look at which flier. "You know there was Bill, but he is dead. There was also Tory who took over my training when Sam went mad. We also met a man named Isaac just before the mountain erupted."

Both James and Roberts turned and looked at Michael as he said this. Clearly this had not come up in any conversations before. "I think there could be more but maybe some of them have died already." It was James who put this into words for everyone. Reality was coming home to roost, again.

"There could have been, but no one else that I met." Michael should have discussed this long ago, but frankly forgot to

Finding the Family of Killers

mention Isaac before. He really didn't intentionally withhold Isaac's name, or at least he didn't think so.

"I agree. There is one with a preference for young girls, and one with a preference for older girls. There may be more." Roberts spoke aloud as he walked the line of fliers and was really speaking more to himself at this point.

"We have a lot of work to do. I'll speak to the mayor about getting you some money if we can." James would have to lay off other officers, but maybe the FBI would kick in a man or two. It was all guess work at this point.

Bobbie Kaald

Bones Surface

As Zeke predicted, the ground around his plants dried and shrank as the plants died and turned brown. He was not there to see this, but the neighborhood feral animals were. As time passed, a pack of dogs got into his former backyard and began making holes for beds and from play and fighting.

As the holes got deeper, bones began to protrude and be spread around the formerly landscaped yard. By the time the neighbors called to complain about the pack of dogs and the authorities arrived to pick some of them up, there was a vast array of human bones and skeletal remains spread all across the back of Zeke's former home.

Finding the Family of Killers

When the authorities arrived, the dogs ran off, but they didn't go more than a few feet on the other side of the bushes. When the investigating officers looked in the back, they called for reinforcements and animal control. They remained close to the back in case the dogs became emboldened enough to try and get back to the bones they were working on.

Late that night, Captain Walters and Sargent Leroy were taking a short break from the crime scene. "We are way over our heads. Has anyone found anything on the man who owns the place?" Walters had collapsed onto a rickety piece of junk lawn chair to drink a quick cup of coffee and asked no one and everyone and anyone who had an answer.

"Yes, we are in over our heads. I sent for the records of this property, but they told me it was in arrears and up on the auction block. I couldn't get a name out of them because they are still trying to track him down and send him a notice. The story goes on and on. I am certain at this point that any name they come up with is fictitious." Leroy blurted out his findings and came to a stop as he downed his cold coffee.

"So. I don't suppose you remember where the information on that FBI guy who was working on the missing persons cases, not too long ago, is?" Walters was ready to dump this case on anyone, and they were only half of a day into it.

Bobbie Kaald

"Not a bad idea. We can turn this all over to the FBI. We are close to the border with Canada. If any of these remains came from there, it is the FBI's case." Leroy tossed his cup in their garbage for non-crime related items. "Maybe you should just call the FBI with an inquiry and let them decide. We do not have the personnel needed for this humongous disaster." He turned and walked back over to see if he could help with anything.

Sighing heavily, Walters leaned forward and stood up with a great deal of difficulty. He turned and left to find his car. He needed to get back to the office and call the FBI. When he got there, he intended to find that contact number for the team who were searching for the men involved in a similar case when the volcano erupted and put a stop to everything else.

As Walters walked back through the house, it struck him as being just the same as when he made his safety check years ago. He stopped for a minute and looked around. A creepy feeling began to come over him. It was like this man moved into someone else's home and never changed a thing. He shook his head and walked to the front door where an officer stood guard. "No one touches anything in the house until I get back."

With that, Walters walked away from the scene as he saw animal control still trying to round up all of the dog pack for testing. "This is a total zoo." He spoke under his breath as he tried for find solutions to some of the massive problems they were staring at now that the dogs dug up the yard.

Finding the Family of Killers

A Spark

Elsewhere in the State, a group of teenagers were having a campout. It was into day two and a party had started a couple of hours after breakfast when the teenagers began to dance and carry their drink with them.

None of the teenagers thought anything about the dryness of the grass in the field. They were simply happy to have found a field to camp on that was blocked from view of cars driving by. As they danced around the fire someone built, one of the boys threw another log on the fire and sparks flew up into the smoke billowing up into the sky.

The sun was going down and the sparks were hypnotizing. The dancers stopped and watched the sparks go up. As the

Bobbie Kaald

sparks rose up into the updraft, they began to blink out. One particularly large piece of ash had many sparks clinging to it. It only rose up about half as far as the others and then it started to fall back to the earth. The wind was blowing in ever changing directions as it will around a fire and the piece of ash with its sparks was nearing the ground. Still three sparks were flaming in tiny flickering lights.

When the burning piece of ash touched the dry dead grass, the sparks lit the grass on fire. Smoke immediately began to rise into the air followed by flames that grew quickly and began moving across the field. No one moved for a seemingly long period of time and then everyone was kicking dirt onto the fire from wherever they stood. One boy's pants began to smoke. He moved away from the fire and bent over to throw dirt on his pants.

The air was hot and dry and the flames threatened to climb into the sky. The size of the party helped with this. Even though they had been drinking, the teenagers followed the movements of their team captain. The flames were soon down, and the adrenaline lessened. When the activity began to slow down, a snapping sound was heard as someone stepped down on the dirt to keep the flames smothered.

Once again everyone who heard the sound stopped moving. All eyes went to the ground to see what had caused the noise. "These are bones, not branches, that we kicked up." A boy

Finding the Family of Killers

announced and a couple of girls screamed. Everyone began to run for their cars. They were over-reacting because none of them wanted their parents to know they were partying.

"I will stay and make certain the flames stay gone. One of you needs to go to the police station." The boy who identified the bones yelled at the backs of his retreating friends. He hoped someone would send him help. In the meantime, he continued to put out the fire in the pit and watch the grass for flames and smoke.

Stan paced around full of ever building anxiety even after the smoke and heat were gone. He moved to the edge of the bushes and away from where they heard the cracking sound. It seemed like it was nearly morning before anyone came to see what the commotion was all about.

Stan knew that his car was blocking the entrance to the clearing, but he forgot to move it. When he heard a car entering the narrow passage, he forced his way around his car and began walking out the way he drove in. He wanted to get this over with because he felt like he was already asleep but walking.

"Are you the one who called to report finding bones?" The lead officer called to Stan who stopped in his tracks in confusion.

"Ah, no, but I stayed to help you find them. There is no reception here." Stan answered. "It's a tight fit, but if you follow me to the other side of my car. We were having a party, and everything was going great. We started dancing and then someone put too much wood on the fire. The ashes started the

162

Bobbie Kaald

dead grass on fire, and we had to kick dirt on the burning grass. We did get the fire out, but something cracked really loud and everyone ran away." Stan finished talking as he passed his car. He moved to the side and remained on the edge of the field.

"Can we turn on your headlights, just for a look see?" The lead officer asked and looked back at his car.

"Sure, but the sun will be up soon." Stan remained standing but moved further to the side to allow the headlight to do its thing.

"You need to unlock the car." The officer said and waited.

Stan did so with his high-priced electronic device to unlock doors and many other things. The button also turned on the lights because he left them on when he shut the door. "The lights are on, sir."

"Oh, so they are. Thanks. New fangled gadgets." The officer turned around to look at the field and stopped just as Stan had stopped. He stood at the edge of the field and saw not one but many white bones sticking up into the air from where they had been buried.

After a long pause, the officer turned to Stan. "I need you to come down to the station tomorrow and give a statement. If you could ask the others at the party to come in at their convenience, I would appreciate it. No one is under suspicion in any way, but I just need to know about the bone discovery."

Finding the Family of Killers

"Is there any way that I can get my car out?" Stan asked as he could see the many cars behind his car.

It took a minute for the officer to respond, and then he said, "Walk out to the last officer and tell him the Captain said for you to be taken home. Give me your car keys and I will return your car later today." He knew the officer would get the address when he dropped the boy off at home.

Stan's mouth dropped open to respond and then he sighed and cut off his response because he couldn't see any other way for him to get to bed sometime today. He turned and began walking out. His sole goal right now was to get to his bed before he collapsed.

Bobbie Kaald

James

While Michael was busy in the basement, the fax machine began spitting out notifications non-stop near twenty-four hours a day. At first, James just continued with the usual copy and file and send one copy downstairs. It was a slow and tedious process with all the other jobs of phone answering and of course, people coming inside to file complaints or needs.

Eventually, James started to pile up the faxes in an in box and when he copied them; they went into his files and Michael's box. It was then that he began to see that the number of incoming faxes was increasing.

Finding the Family of Killers

The next time that Michael came up to see James there were so many new faxes that he staggered back when he saw them. "James, where did these come from?"

"I haven't been able to sort through them and I want you to do that up here so we can find out if they are coming from the same area, or what is going on." James was at his end trying to manage the police station and manage these victim's fliers. He didn't want them coming back on this side of the mountains and he needed help.

"I talked to Roberts this morning. He is currently at the local FBI headquarters trying to inform them that the case is ongoing and even bigger than we knew of before." Michael spoke as he carried the fliers over to the table he used for sorting and began sorting by the area the notification came from. Right now, he was planning on sorting by Northwest, Northeast, Southwest, and Southeast. He would maintain this plan unless it became apparent that a group of them were from the same office.

It only took about a minute to decide that most of the fliers were from the northeast quadrant. Michael finished sorting the fliers once and then stacked the other three sections with two fliers a piece off to the side without mixing them together.

The second time through, Michael went slower. He looked at all their headers and tried to find which city was involved. He memorized the cities and their locations the best that he was able when he studied for his GED. Still, there were cities that he

Bobbie Kaald

found confusing as to where on the map they lay. Some of them sounded so much alike.

By the time Michael finished, there were ten more fliers on the fax machine. He already knew there was a problem in one particular county and took the new fliers into James office. He stopped just inside of the doorframe until James finished his current call. When James hung up, Michael spoke. "Someone is killing or has killed in central Okanagan County."

"I came to that conclusion as well. I just needed a second opinion." James reached for the phone to call the Okanagan County Sheriff's office. He just got off the phone with Pend Oreille County Sheriff's office. They just found a field of skeletal remains. "I will come down and compare notes when I finish this call."

Michael shrugged his shoulders and returned to the sorting pile. He returned all four piles spread out on the table, and then sorted the new fliers into his piles. When he finished this, he made copies of each pile and placed his copies off to the side. He then filed the originals in the office files.

Picking up his copies, Michael headed toward the basement to begin making sense of them. He long since decided that he needed a bigger room. He hoped the FBI would agree to help.

Finding the Family of Killers

Help

Roberts returned home two days later and went directly to James office. When he entered, James wasn't in his office. "Is James down in the basement?" He spoke aloud so all those on duty could hear.

"No, he isn't, but he said you should look in the basement when you arrived, sir." The officer was about to answer the phone but spoke to Roberts briefly before turning to the phone.

Roberts nodded and walked to the back of the building. He tried the door, but it was locked. Using his key, he let himself into the basement and descended the stairs quickly continuing across the room to the desks. There was a note with his name on it laying on the one closest to him. He picked it up and read

Bobbie Kaald

it. It was brief and to the point. Michael and James were driving to the far edge of Washington due a field of skeletal remains being found and reported.

Roberts lay the note back on the desk and looked around. Without a doubt this room was not big enough. He had to go back upstairs to use the phone because their line was not yet hooked up. 'I should have pushed them harder. We need the FBI back in on this case.' Roberts was thinking this hard and wishing that he had not yet retired.

Roberts walked into James' office and shut the door. Sitting down behind James desk felt a little weird, but he picked up the phone and dialed the FBI switchboard. When the voice mail came on, he pushed in his code and waited.

"Hello." The director who Roberts spoke with earlier today answered. His voice was distinctively deep with a slight scratch to it.

"This is Roberts. I just got back to James office. There is a field of skeletal remains in Eastern Washington. James and Michael have driven over there. I recommend setting up a portable warehouse type morgue close by the field." Roberts answered directly since he knew the office was about to close. "It is close to the border of Canada and Idaho. Yes, I think we may need two field tent set-ups. Yes, I think it is more than one body. It might be more than ten sets of remains."

Finding the Family of Killers

Roberts began to leaf through the paper left strewn on James desk. It was never this disorganized. Michael must have found something big for them to take off like this. As he listened to the other side of the conversation, he picked up a bunch of faxes. The one sitting on the top told the story. "Excuse me, sir. Apparently, there are two areas, one each in different towns, filled with many skeletal remains."

Roberts listened some more and then hung up. He would be receiving two teams. He needed to pack a big to go bag and shower, not in that order. This said case was going to be a long investigation just like last time. At least he was being paid as a consultant, the pay was better. He wouldn't have an expense account, but he was already receiving a retirement check. This would balance out for him if he didn't pig out at meals.

An hour later, Roberts stopped for a to go dinner from the local hand-out. It was getting late in the day, but he ordered enough for several meals. It took at least twenty minutes for his order and there were cars behind him out into the street.

After exchanging money and food, Roberts put the bags on the passenger seat and rolled up his window as he slowly began driving away from the drive-by window. It was a tedious entry to the main road but part of it was built twenty or thirty years before the rest and everything was connected. It was a matter

Bobbie Kaald

of letting everyone else have the right of way to save one's sanity and life. Not to mention the drivability of his car.

    Finally, Roberts made a safe left onto the main road leading out of town toward the mountains and the unknown fields. He thought about heading for the airport in Eastern Washington first, but he wouldn't have any idea what the flights would be. They were on their own to find the two fields. He did fax the two fliers to the FBI office before leaving. He just wished he knew for certain where James and Michael went. They needed to split up at least for the start of this investigation.

Finding the Family of Killers

Zeke's yard

James and Michael pulled into town after midnight. James parked in front of the police station and saw that Michael was asleep when he looked at him. There were no lights inside of the station, for that reason James leaned back and closed his eyes as well. Morning would be soon enough for them to look at the skeletal remains. This is one thing they all learned on the prolonged case not so long ago. Nothing is stat, and nothing can't wait until tomorrow. Skeletal usually meant long dead and not going anywhere.

James felt like he just got to sleep when he heard someone knocking. "James, an officer wants you to open your door."

Bobbie Kaald

Michael was shaking James shoulder and trying to wake James up. James only moaned.

Michael gave up and got out on his own side. "The sleeping officer is James Johnson. I'm Michael. I have previously been abducted by these men. We got a fax and drove over to see the skeletal remains you discovered." Michael spoke quickly to keep the officer from interrupting and then he would forget to tell the entire story.

"I am the officer on duty. I think we should let him sleep. Why don't you come in and have some coffee? Nothing can be done until morning." The officer walked over to the office door as he spoke and unlocked it. He entered without another word and went about making new coffee for what would be another long day.

Michael followed along behind in a state of fear. He had never worked with a police officer who was new to him, and he was not an officer. He was a recently released man from parole who had killed a woman even if it was an accident. He took the liberty of sitting down and remained silent to wait for the officer to speak first.

When the officer had the pot filled with water, he walked over and took a seat behind the desk. "You read the fax?"

"I did. I'm in charge of setting up a system of sorting through faxes. Most of them are from missing women. One had a boy whose mother was killed. We are trying to find the boy before

Finding the Family of Killers

they scar him emotionally into one of them." Michael spelled it out for this officer who probably had no idea how many men were involved. Michael didn't have that answer either, but he only wanted to save the boy.

"We have teams uncovering the bodies we found. Turns out there are more than ten." The officer's face was frozen into stone and seemed to be close to breaking down.

"This is new for you, isn't it?" Michael asked.

"I have been involved in murders before, but never to this scale." The officer admitted and got up to pour them both a mug of coffee. "Black?"

"Yes, that's fine." Michael accepted the coffee and found himself wishing that James were awake.

The officer returned to his chair and remained silent for a long time. "None of the bones have been removed so far. We have only been uncovering the graves."

"There is another man, Roberts, who will be coming. He is a retired FBI agent. I left him a note. He is making arrangements for the FBI to become involved again." Michael tried not to release information that he shouldn't. It was difficult because he had no real training, only guidance from his two rescuers. He paused and sipped slowly at his coffee as if the cold fluid were still too hot to drink.

"Well, that is good news because we have a real mess here." The officer stopped talking suddenly and got up to hurry away into the bathroom.

Bobbie Kaald

Michael felt sorry for the officer. He remembered crying one night during the first year of his captivity. He cried all night long but by morning he had accepted his new terrible life and vowed never to cry again. He had never cried since that awful night, but many times he felt the need to.

The door opened as the officer returned and sat back down. James walked in. "Michael, you should have woken me when the officer came." He didn't realize that they tried to do just that.

"That's funny." Michael said as he got up to fill his coffee cup up again. "You probably want some coffee?"

"That would be a grand idea, black. My name is James, and I suppose Michael has been filling you in while I slept." James walked over and offered his hand to the officer.

"My boss will be in when it gets light out. They worked until dark uncovering the graves." The officer didn't want to repeat everything because it really upset him. "My name is Sargent Chose. My boss' name is Captain Helm. Michael has been filling me in on another man coming later?"

"We hope he is on his way. He was at the FBI headquarters informing them that the killing had not stopped." James took a drink of his coffee and decided that he didn't need to add anything. He carried it over to the only other chair in the place and sat down. "Is there a motel or room to rent?"

Finding the Family of Killers

"I will call around after seven." Sargent Chose answered as he also got up to fill up his coffee cup. He was thinking to himself that this was going to be an extremely long day. "I'm certain we can find you some place to stay. This may take months to sift through." He spoke brokenly as if unable to find the right words.

James looked at Michael and they both nodded. They knew what this young officer was feeling. James stood up and walked back to the officer before answering. "Thank-you for your help. If you could inform your superior of our arrival, we will wait in the car in case Roberts drives up. We can watch for his car better outside." James adlibbed his excuse to leave for the officer's sake. He shook hands and placed his empty coffee cup on the desk. "Thank you for the coffee, it is just what I needed." With that, he turned and walked toward the door.

Michael got up and put his empty coffee cup on the desk. He walked quickly to the where he assumed the bathroom was and a minute or so later, he walked out of the office. Once outside, he saw that James was back in the car with the door shut. Following his example, Michael returned to the passenger seat. When the door shut, he looked at James and asked. "What are we doing back in the car?"

"That young man is out of his comfort zone and I just wanted to give him some time alone without having to entertain us until he is relieved." James leaned his seat back a half of an inch. "I shouldn't have driven the cruiser. My personal car would be

Bobbie Kaald

more comfortable, but I didn't want to risk any of our needs contaminating it." James closed his eyes as he spoke and the memory of the smell in his cruiser's trunk overwhelmed his mind enough to make him very nauseous. No dead bodies in his personal car, ever again.

Finding the Family of Killers

Roberts arrives

Roberts drove most of the way in the dark. His lights barely made a difference when the fog rolled in from the river down in the canyon somewhere in the dark. He forgot about the bridge and nearly rolled his car as he slowed on the slippery roadway for the turn.

After the bridge, the fog cleared away and he was able to make better time. By the time Roberts reached here, he had decided to stop at the first town with a reported discovery of bones in a yard. He wouldn't stay long if James and Michael already arrived there. He would just compare notes and move onto the address of the next flier. In any case, he would need to gas up his car before continuing onto the border.

Bobbie Kaald

The sun was just coming up when Roberts entered the town. Driving slowly down the main street, he was struck by how much this town looked like the other Eastern Washington towns. They were all built about the same era and never improved or changed. A car backed out and revealed James car parked in front of the police station.

Roberts laughed and parked right away. He got out and shut his door quietly. Approaching James car, he knew that he was right. James lay back with his eyes closed. Michael was also laying back with his eyes closed. Roberts made it all the way up to James car and nearly knocked when an officer exited the station.

"Do you need something?" The officer asked and instantly James and Michael were awake.

"I have just arrived, and they are expecting me." Roberts felt instant guilt at his almost accomplished act of tomfoolery. "I am a retired FBI agent and brought them news."

"We are expecting you. I am off duty now but will be back later. My boss is inside waiting for the three of you." With that Sargent Chose turned and walked away.

James and Michael exited their car simultaneously. "I believe that is our cue to see the man." James spoke but never stopped moving.

"After we view the site, I am leaving to check on the other site. Teams of FBI agents and investigators are on their way. As

Finding the Family of Killers

I drove over here, I was thinking we should try to find a place halfway between the two sites for the portable tents. We don't have enough help to have two sites." Roberts finished speaking as they opened the door to the office.

James entered last and Michael followed Roberts inside. Roberts walked over to the Captain's desk before speaking. "I am Roberts, the said retired FBI man that James was waiting for."

"I'm glad you arrived because I need to head over to the property to monitor their progress finding those grisly remains." The Captain stood up and put on his coat. "We should take two cars because you will want to leave before me, I suppose."

"You're right about that. I will take a quick look see and then leave for the other site. Other investigators will arrive shortly." Roberts moved back to allow the Captain to proceed them.

"Other site? Never mind, I don't really want to know. I have my hands full with this one." With that said the Captain stopped talking and walked out. He waited for the others to leave and then shut and locked the station door.

Everyone got into their cars without further conversation. Each was wondering what the Sheriff meant by 'grisly' remains. Each was hoping for a fully decomposed skeleton but couldn't stop thinking about the smell of a newly decomposing corpse.

Bobbie Kaald

As it turned out, Roberts did not leave for more than a day. The other officers arrived, and they took over the investigation. When Roberts reminded them of a second site, they asked the town Captain to call around to see if there was a field they could rent for a portable morgue between here and the Idaho border.

The Captain walked away from his field of discovery, and Roberts remained there for an hour or more before driving back to the police station. He parked and walked inside to see if the Captain had any luck. "I thought I would see if you needed any help." He spoke as he entered and then stopped when he saw the Captain hold up his hand and point at the phone receiver in his other hand.

Roberts took a seat next to the coffee pot and waited. Of course, he helped himself to a cup of coffee while he waited. As he sipped on the coffee, he tried not to listen on the Captain's part of the phone call. He heard most of it anyway.

"Sorry about that. I found a property owner willing to let you use his field for free because of what you will be helping to put a stop to." The Captain got up while he spoke and walked over to where Roberts was sitting. He handed Roberts a piece of paper. "I would drive you up there, but someone needs to tend to the regular police work that has gone by the wayside with the discovery of the remains."

Finding the Family of Killers

"I understand completely, James will be returning to the coast soon. I think Michael will go with him because he needs to retrieve the mass of fliers he has accumulated. I asked for him to just copy them and leave the investigation room the way it is. We will be using it when we are on the coast." Roberts threw away his cup and stood up. "I need to get on the road. Can you tell me where to find this field?"

After getting directions, Roberts drove back to where he left James and Michael. All the way he was running things though his head about how to handle the next few days. He wanted Michael to feel good about his position in this case. The FBI didn't want Michael interfering, and this put Roberts in a bad position. Only time would tell if he could make the correct decisions for both sides of the issue.

Bobbie Kaald

Phillip

Phillip did not bring up going to school and neither did anyone else. He remained upstairs most of the time and read books the three men brought him. He remained quiet out of habit from a lifetime of abuse. Smiling when people came to see him was not easy and he did flinch when people reached out for him. Fortunately, the men were not touchy/feely people either and didn't notice that Phillip flinched if touched.

Phillip listened to the comings and goings downstairs but wasn't curious enough to go downstairs and investigate. After dark, Tory called him down to join them and Phillip went to see if there was anything to eat, he hoped. There was.

Finding the Family of Killers

"Phillip, come and eat." Tory greeted him as per usual, but his voice held a tone of uneasiness.

"Thanks, I am hungry." Phillip sat down and began eating. He didn't know that many kids would ask what they were being served. He knew it brought trouble at home to do so, and he continued that behavior here. As far as Phillip was concerned, silence was indeed golden.

While Phillip ate, Tory sat down across from him. "We need to leave after you eat." Normally, he would just announce it, but Isaac volunteered to keep Phillip here.

"Just us, or everyone?" Phillip asked shyly and cringed as he thought Tory would be angry that he even asked.

Tory answered quickly without even realizing that Phillip was scared. "Just us. We can go back to a hole that I have by the mountains and as far as anyone else is concerned just say that your mother is my sister. She left you with me for a month because she is having surgery. Are you good with that?"

Phillip smiled and nodded. He couldn't answer with his mouth full of the cheeseburger Tory brought him.

"You can answer when your mouth is empty." Tory smiled but was not willing to take a nod. "I need you to answer because Isaac says that you can stay here."

"If you're going, I want to go." Phillip trusted Tory because he saved him, but he barely knew any of the other men.

Bobbie Kaald

"That makes it unanimous. We both want you to go." Tory got up and picked up his left-over dishes and took them to the garbage. Phillip was right behind him.

"Can I take my things?" Phillip asked. He had never moved without leaving everything behind before.

"You need your books and paper. I got you a box to keep them in, didn't I?" Tory was confused now. "Is it too heavy for you?"

"I don't think so." Phillip turned and ran to the stairs and over to his room.

Tory followed along to make certain that Phillip could carry the box without falling down the stairs. He watched as Phillip struggled to pick up his box and leaned over to take it from him. "You can carry it next time, Phillip."

"I'll go and open the door for you." Phillip ran on ahead and good to his word, he opened the door and closed it behind them. In the back of his mind he wondered where Isaac, Zeke, and Lane were.

Finding the Family of Killers

The Morgue

Roberts spent his days and nights on the road now. He had two excavation sites miles apart and an investigation tent and morgue tent in a field of humongous boulders reportedly from space. He also had a room with all of their fliers for the missing girls six hours away on the other side of the mountain. He had never been a party to such a comedy of disaster.

"Michael, I'm here at a fax machine. I texted you the number and thought you could send me the copies of your latest fliers." Roberts drove over and made copies of all the other files right after the FBI started to set up the two tents. Two or three times a week he called Michael for the new ones.

Bobbie Kaald

"I was just going to call you. There are three new fliers from the small town just south of you. You will see when the fax finishes spitting out the fliers. I'll call you if I find any new connections." Michael finished speaking and then the line went dead. He had hung up to get back to work.

As Roberts put the phone down, the fax next to him began to spit out fliers, as Michael would say. Roberts leaned up against the counter to wait for the fliers to finish coming out and then took them over and paid for the use of the fax machine. He needed a weekend off to rest. Already he could feel his age creeping in and taking his energy away. He retired for a reason and this was just a consultation case. Logging that away in the back of his mind, Roberts walked out of the copying store and into the sunlight as he headed for his car.

Once inside his car, Roberts drove out of the parking area and headed for the twin tents as he thought of them. He knew how large an area that they eventually needed before and this made him fight for an equally large area for this team. He would turn over these fliers and then find some food and bed. It would be late by then and too late to drive home safely tonight.

Arriving at the turn off into the investigation sight, Roberts parked and got out. He forgot the fliers in the car and went back for them. If he was this tired, he felt that he made the correct decision to drive home in the morning. It was nearly a six-hour

Finding the Family of Killers

drive from here, but he was ready to go home and sleep on his own bed.

Entering, Roberts stopped after his first step inside the tent. His eyes slowly adjusted to the loss of glare and he pushed his sunglasses up onto the top of his head. Before him was a scene beyond description. Tarps on the floor with taped off areas for each set of identified bones. "What the ………." He just broke off verbalizing and knew this was another man's mess. Keeping his disapproval to himself would be difficult but necessary.

Continuing his walk in, Roberts looked at all of the workers and eventually found the man in charge. "Lieutenant, I brought you the next set of missing person fliers found to be of significance for you to help identify your remains."

"Always glad for your help. What are your plans from here?" the recently made Lieutenant asked. He was not smiling as he took the wad of fliers from Roberts. "We need to get these guys soon. They have been killing an enormous number of innocent women over the years. Do you even know how many men are involved?"

"I am thinking four or five judging from the age groups of the missing. One man drove off the top of the pass and is dead not long ago. My housemate, Michael, was a captive of the group and he only knows of two more, but I think these two graveyards indicate at least two more." Roberts was anxious to leave but needed to answer the man as honestly as he could.

Bobbie Kaald

"That many? Do you think they are living together or separately?" The Lieutenant asked almost under his breath.

"We have evidence from our past investigation that they move around. No one can answer that except maybe Michael, and I haven't asked." Roberts answered in an off-hand remark but followed with closure. "I am headed home and will be certain to ask him that very thing. Be certain to request missing persons reports for up to seventy-five years ago from all the surrounding counties and provinces."

After dropping the big bomb, Roberts turned and left. He didn't need to look back because he was certain that the Lieutenant was experiencing the stunned silence of overwhelm. He felt that way a lot when he ran his investigation.

Finding the Family of Killers

West Coast Central

Michael brought breakfast and coffee along with him every day now and took it directly into his new independent study office. He was trying to maintain a positive attitude, but he was having a lot of trouble keeping it up. He was obsessed with them having a new abductee to groom. This caused him to be depressed underneath his new façade for his friends.

He placed all the new fliers up every morning and afternoon. They hung around the room with accusative eyes. After a few hours down in the pit alone, Michael went upstairs for a break with living beings.

Bobbie Kaald

On Michael's third trip upstairs for the day, Roberts pulled into the parking in front of the station having just arrived from Eastern Washington. Michael didn't see him because he was over at the fax machine collecting his newest fliers. As he turned around to head for his sorting table, Roberts walked in.

"Michael, I was hoping you hadn't gone to dinner yet." Roberts tried to keep his voice light as if he were smiling.

Michael looked up when he heard his name. "Roberts, I'm glad that you're back and no, I haven't eaten. I am ready to leave for today because I just can't think any more."

"Sorry about that, do you need to get anything downstairs?" Roberts knew it was a big step for Michael to admit that he was stressed out.

"Just let me put these fliers on my table and I am ready. James already went home." Michael quickly put his fliers on the table and a stapler on top to keep them there. On second thought, he walked back and locked the basement door before joining Roberts in his car.

"I thought we could go out to eat tonight. Fill me in on your thoughts while I drive." Roberts backed out and turned to head for the main road and then on into the next town. He continued talking as he drove. "The new director at the investigation tent wants to know how many killers there are."

Finding the Family of Killers

"All I know, you know. There is Tory and Isaac from before and of course the new boy. I suppose there is a new man responsible for each of the boneyards. I guess that makes four." Michael came up with the same answer Roberts gave and this made Roberts smile.

"That is just what I said." Roberts answered back. "Anything new with the fliers?"

"I found some of the old fliers. It seems a bunch of women went missing over the years down by Isaac's bakery. I guess that I should have looked into that before." Michael responded and went silent.

Roberts took this as a message that they would talk more later. After dinner would be a good time after Michael was rested and fed. He still hadn't asked if Michael thought the men lived together or not.

Bobbie Kaald

Volcanic Ash

As with all present and past capitalists, it didn't take long for the entrepreneurs to begin making use of the ash laying all around the southwestern fourth of Washington State. Ash lay over everything and the clean up was on going. Once the streets were clear, every windstorm coated the roads again.

Eventually, the loose ash was hardened by the rain and stayed where it was put. That's when the entrepreneurs began taking more than a little of it home with them. They made souvenirs and some began making glass.

Finding the Family of Killers

At this time, collecting ash was a megalithic construction enterprise. Currently, a contractor was beginning an excavation of an open area just southeast of the abandoned bakery. If Isaac knew about it, he would break out in a sweat and turn white as a ghost.

First bulldozer load of dirt seemed like ash and billowed up into the air now that the hardened surface was broken. With the second load of soil and ash, it was a different story. As the load poured forth from the scoop into the truck, white stick like things clung to the scoop and the operator stopped pouring and moved the yellow construction loader back a little.

The operator began shouting incoherently as he tried to climb down to examine what was literally sticking out of the dirt and debris in his scoop. "Wake up the boss and get him over here!" He jumped the last five feet down and took five running steps to the front. Grabbing the white stick, he pulled it and a partial skeleton came with it. A human skull was attached. It slid from his hands an fell the rest of the way to the hardened ash crust at his feet shattering on impact.

"Shut everything down and call the police." The operator spoke loudly as he walked over to the operator's shack. He saw the crew's boss exiting and continued walking.

"Why are you shutting things down? We just started." The boss, Jeff, tried not to yell but he was feeling really angry. They

Bobbie Kaald

needed to get this done. He almost went bankrupt when the volcano blew up and shut everything down.

"I just dug up a human skeleton." The obviously shaken operator answered. "We need to call the police."

"Send everyone home for the day. It will take hours to get the county sheriff to make an entrance." Jeff turned around and kicked the trailer before opening the door and disappearing inside.

"Jeff says for everyone to go home. I will be staying with the excavator for now." The operator, Jed, said to everyone as he walked back to his mess and climbed back inside of the cab to stay warm and dry for the next four or five hours before the sheriff arrived.

He leaned back after shutting the cab door and closed his eyes. Seemingly seconds later, Jeff was knocking on the shovel. When Jed opened his eyes, he saw Jeff motioning for him to lower the shovel.

"Let me know when I am too close to the skull." Jed closed the door and cranked up the engine to his excavator. After a full sixty second warm up, he slowly lowered the scoop down for Jeff to look inside. Jed watched Jeff for cues, but none came. When he knew it was almost too low, Jed stopped the downward motion and turned off the engine. Climbing down, Jed walked up to where a now pale Jeff stood.

Finding the Family of Killers

"We are going to have to choose a different site." Jeff said and walked around Jed and headed back to the trailer.

Jed stepped back as his boss left. Then he stepped over to see what Jeff was talking about. Looking down into the scoop, Jed saw that it was filled with human skeletons. The one on the ground was only partial and the rest was somewhere. Jed counted skulls and knew in his heart that there were seven or eight just in this small scrapping. He didn't even want to know how many more were laying under the surface of this open space. He really hoped these people didn't die from the eruption of the volcano.

Bobbie Kaald

Another Field

Roberts was home packing for a return trip to find out how many skeletal remains were found in each field. He locked the house as he took out his last load. Next stop, the police station to collect any fliers to take. He put the load in and closed he trunk. Two steps put him at the driver's door, and he was inside.

The engine roared to life and Roberts put on his sunglasses because the sun was on the downward quarter of the day. He drove the short two blocks to the main street and stopped to wait for an opening. When the opening came, he gunned it across and braked to park.

Finding the Family of Killers

Roberts got out quickly because he was in a hurry to get going. One of these trips, he needed to leave at dawn. In three steps, he was opening the door and heard James shocked voice coming out of his office. "What kind of bones? Human skulls? We will be down in a couple of hours." With that he hung up the phone loudly without meaning to. "Roberts, I thought you left. You might want to call and tell them you will be delayed for two days."

Roberts sat down because he had heard enough to know this was bad news. "Give it to me, where and how many."

James looked him in the eye. "I believe it is Isaac's burial site. It is down almost to the volcano. They were digging in an ash site and came up with a scoop filled with bones."

"That's several hours south of the ghost town." Roberts was thinking hard and trying to piece it together. "Let's bring a sketch artist with us. If Isaac were seen with a group of men before the mountain blew and afterward, we could get sketches of these men."

"That's a good idea. Michael will be able to do that for us." James announce as he got up to go bring Michael up out of the basement.

Roberts got up and walked out to the fax machine to look for anything new. On top of the pile was one from just where they were heading, 'Field of bones discovered under the ash.' Just lovely, they would have to decide if they were murdered or killed by the ash. In his mind, he knew them to be murdered but

Bobbie Kaald

the public would be wondering and wanting answers. 'No pressure.' He thought to himself as he waited for Michael and James to be ready to go.

"Ready," James asked as he appeared out of the basement. "Michael is right behind me."

"We need to get on the road. There is no quick way there, is there?" Roberts turned and walked out of the office. He wanted to take the cruiser and do lights and sirens, but the victims were long dead not going anywhere. This was turning into a sick slogan for him.

Roberts was inside his own car before he knew it and a minute later James and Michael joined him. "Take the Maple Valley Hiway, it is slow but faster than others?"

"Just drive south to the new freeway and follow the signs." James answered as he read over some of the fliers that he had not seen before.

Roberts backed his car up and headed south as directly as possible. His adrenaline was up. He really should be calling the FBI, but he wanted to get a personal look at the scene before calling.

More than two hours later, Roberts was approaching the site they were given earlier. He felt a sudden urge to turn back when he saw the massive number of vehicles and tents up in

Finding the Family of Killers

front of him. "I think we're here." He sarcastically announced to the car.

"I believe we are. Michael, I want you to wander through the crowd and find out if anyone knew Isaac and if they saw him with other men." James turned around and spoke to Michael. "Take your drawing paper and pencils with you."

Michael was prepared for this, but it still came as a shock when James gave him permission to ask questions, too. "I can do that?"

"Just make certain that you write their answers down, and who told you. You need the name and address off of their driver's license and their phone number if they have one." James answered and opened his car door. He had his uniform on and wished he didn't because someone starched it and it was rubbing him raw.

Roberts and James walked over to the scene and Michael began mingling in the crowd. Just once, Michael looked back at his two friends to make certain he had not heard wrong. They were not looking at him and Michael smiled and began working the crowd.

Roberts ducked under the crime scene tape and walked up to the start of the dig. It did resemble an archeologic dig because people were down on their hands and knees brushing the dirt and debris away. The also had high quality masks on to keep from inhaling the ash that was now flying around, again.

Bobbie Kaald

"Who is in charge here?" Roberts spoke loudly to let his voice carry above the work noise. James stood beside Roberts and was just speechless at the size of this excavation. When he looked up there were small excavations every two feet across a large field and about ten small excavations across. He was feeling greatly relieved not to be more involved with this site than he was.

No one responded for a long time, but finally a man turned and motioned for them to come over to where he was standing next to a table. Roberts nodded and began walking along the edge of the field toward where the man was.

James began looking around at the uncovered dump sites. All he saw were skeletal remains. A couple of the investigators seemed to have evidence bags with small items in them. When he saw this, he walked around to where Roberts was talking to the man in charge. "Roberts, some of these remains have personal items buried with them."

"More than a few. Some have full backpacks buried with them. The personal items aren't just necklaces. We need to get back and make a list of personal items that are listed on the fliers." Roberts filled in what he knew to be true.

"Does that mean that more than one killer was using this field at some time?" James asked because he was certain this was true.

Finding the Family of Killers

"Maybe, I need to get out of here and contact the local FBI office." Roberts moved around James to start walking away when the man behind him cleared his throat. Roberts turned around and looked him in the eye.

"That won't be necessary. We contacted them as soon as the first bone was found. I know about all the killings over the years and I read the fliers from east of the mountains." The officer in charge informed them. "They should be here soon."

James stepped forward and introduced himself. "I am Officer Johnson, and this is Roberts. He is now retired from the FBI. We worked the first part of this case."

"Sorry, I should have introduced myself right away. Captain Stewart at your service." The captain reached out and shook hands with James.

"If they are coming, we will wait to brief them because we have two full teams of investigators involved in those Eastern Washington sites." Roberts announced. "We have an assistant who is organizing hundreds of missing person files as we speak."

"Hundreds?" Stewart looked suddenly paler than before.

"I am afraid so. We were set up before and waited but they all seemed to disappear. I boxed everything up and put it in storage as a cold case with multiple victims. We identified some but many were still awaiting identities." Roberts minced his words and answered to the best of his abilities.

Bobbie Kaald

"The FBI has arrived. Let's go over to them and brief them." Stewart smiled and tried to keep it together long enough to turn this mess over to them.

"After you, sir. You are in charge here." James smiled back because he knew this man was undoubtedly running on overwhelm.

Finding the Family of Killers

Tory and Phillip

Tory and Phillip drove from Isaac's straight through to Tory's safe house after leaving the two men behind. Tory pulled in to check for possible occupants. "Stay here. I will be just a minute and then we'll go and have something to eat."

"Okay, Tory." Phillip preferred to wait anyway just in case something bad was inside of the house.

"I thought you were going to call me Uncle Tory. Remember, my sister is having an operation and you are staying with me for a couple of weeks." Tory added the last part to help build the story. "Some people in town might remember me. It's only been a month or so since I was here."

Bobbie Kaald

"Right, Uncle Tory." Phillip was feeling calmer than he could ever remember and smiled at Tory. He was happy to be with him because the absence of his mother made him happier than he ever thought possible.

Tory turned around without further conversation and walked up to the door. It wasn't locked and he didn't expect it to be. Opening the door, Tory walked straight inside and looked around. Everything was just as he left it. Once through and back outside. Shutting the door to the house, Tory was back inside of his car in about five steps through the tall grass. His shoes and pants legs were wet but the heater should dry by the time they reached a place for dinner.

"What's for dinner?" Phillip asked Tory.

"Not much of a choice here on this side of the mountains. I guess you can just call it pot-luck. I just don't think pancakes three times a day is going to be acceptable. Hamburger or hot dog, maybe, okay?" Tory got very tired of the menus in local restaurants. "Maybe we can take a trip across the mountains tomorrow."

With that, Tory backed the car out of the overgrown access road and headed for someplace to eat. It suddenly occurred to him that he needed a blanket and a pillow for the kid. Details were slipping from his mind. Tory wondered if his homicidal tendency might just disappear with his memories.

Finding the Family of Killers

Vincent Arrives

The latest FBI team stood and talked to Roberts, James, and Captain Stewart for a long time. Captain Stewart eventually excused himself and walked around collecting his men and equipment. The FBI team began taking over the collection of bones and evidence. Their photographer was busily taking picture to document the expose sites.

As Captain Stewart's team drove away, a man pulled a large rolling piece of equipment out of a van. Roberts looked at it and knew it to be ground penetrating radar. 'This is going to be a long day.' Roberts thought to himself.

Once the radar got moving over ground not yet opened, it stopped every six to ten feet and a flag was placed. After twenty

Bobbie Kaald

flags had been set, the operator stopped again and turned the machine off. "I need more flags. Anyone have any more flags?"

A man grabbed a bunch of flags and ran them over leap frogging over open sites. He handed them to the man and the man returned to his job.

Everyone was involved in extracting the evidence and failed to see a late arrival until he stood right behind Roberts. "I thought you were retired."

Roberts spun around to greet the speaker. "Vincent! I am so glad you finally came. I need your specialty."

"Sorry, I don't work for you. Not to mention, this is a worse mess than we ever had before." Vincent stood eyeballing the site. "I heard a rumor there are two more fields east and north of here. Is that right?"

"Unfortunately, also Michael has a room full of fliers. We think that besides Tory, there must be at least two other men involved because the graves show two age group at least." Roberts paused and looked at the ground before continuing. "I also need you to know that one of them has a young boy. Probably, this boy is with Tory."

"So, I am guessing we need facial reconstruction from the skulls. Good thing that I brought my camera. Excuse me." Vincent began walking around and taking pictures of the skulls and the skeletal remains for a size reference.

Finding the Family of Killers

Roberts followed along behind Vincent. He talked while Vincent took pictures and they formed a plan. Vincent would have to go over to the other sites when he was finished here and by that time, Roberts would have a place for him to work with his computer genius.

After watching Vincent for a moment, Roberts waved to James. He then met James halfway, "I need to take you home and talk to Michael. We have to form a new plan."

"This have anything to do with Vincent?" James turned and walked out with Roberts as they continued to talk.

"It does. We have three huge excavation sites hours apart. Michael has been collecting fliers and collating them into areas. I want him to start listing jewelry the missing may have been wearing. Anything they may have been carrying that may take longer to disintegrate, etc." Roberts cut off his list as it became too gruesome even for him.

"Something that may be in the grave with the body." James finished off as they reached the car.

Michael was there waiting for them. "Trying to ditch me?"

Roberts smiled and got in to begin the drive home. He didn't respond to the bait, but was glad Michael was ready to leave.

"What did you find out, Michael?" James asked when they were moving once again.

"I found out what survived to help identify the victims. I never knew they buried everything with the body to prevent

Bobbie Kaald

finding them." Michael had tears running down his face but wiped them away as he talked.

Roberts and James remained silent for a time to allow Michael to process his feelings. Roberts finally broke the silence an announced, "I don't know about you guys, but I need a nature call and coffee."

"I can always do coffee, but don't you ever eat." Michael spoke up from the back seat and laughed.

Roberts pulled in and parked. The three friends walked in together leaving work in the car. Long ago they began this mostly because they could not talk shop in a restaurant. They unconsciously did what the band of murderers did, listen for information from those around them.

Back on the move again, James was driving at his insistence. "Michael, now that you know what is left to help with identification, use the fliers and compile a list of known items that might help. Vincent will join you after he is finished with photos of all the sites. That will give you time." James spoke softly and tried to cover what he knew.

"Most of the fliers have a phone number to contact. Do you feel up to calling now that you have an extension?" Roberts brought up the rest and left it up to Michael.

Finding the Family of Killers

"I can try, but I don't have people skills and you two know that. I think it would be better if Roberts made those calls." Michael was beginning to know his strengths and weaknesses after taking his courses at college.

"I can do that, but you need to listen to the calls. Basically, we can do them together. I will make the calls on speaker and you can write down what they tell us. I have a separate fax line being set up to allow us a number to give everyone. I plan to ask for pictures of items to be faxed to us if they have them." Roberts was on a role now. They needed to identify and located these men as soon as possible.

James took over with a new idea. "What if I ask the mayor to have a media op. We can ask everyone with any missing persons to make the list and fax it into your number. Won't that speed things up and make it easier for you. I think many people have heard about the excavations and are frantic to help in any way they can."

"Okay, that is all good and on you then." Roberts didn't want to be involved as a retired FBI agent. He looked at James and saw that his poker face was on. This meant that James would talk about it later.

Bobbie Kaald

Breakfast Reveal

Isaac, Zeke, and Lane continued with their habit of eating dinner at their local restaurant slash hash place. After ordering, the three men sipped their coffee and traded sections of the local newspaper.

Zeke was the first to see the article revealing a backyard filled with graves being discovered. The picture was small and the article short. No names were given but the FBI was clearly involved as the back of the vest on people in the photo attested to. "Oh, boys, we have a problem." With that, he handed his piece of the paper to Lane.

Finding the Family of Killers

Lane looked at the article briefly before passing it to Isaac. "It was destined to happen."

Isaac read the entire article. "Well, it looks like all three of us will be under the looking glass of scrutiny."

The food came and they ate in silence. Zeke took the paper when they left. It would only prevent anyone who overheard them from knowing which article they were talking about. They drove back to Isaac's in silence, each lost in their own thoughts.

Once inside, with the door closed, the three sat up late in the night discussing their options. In the end, they decided that any sudden change right after the article was in the paper would be a red flag. None of them looked much alike. Isaac's graveyard was miles from his bakery, and no one would pick up on the connection. The property was state land and not in his name or his pseudonym.

Lane's yard was now state property. He owned it at one time but had not paid any property tax for more than twenty years. There was only a slim possibility of linking the graveyard to him but only through old property records that were in a warehouse somewhere and not computerized.

Zeke was the real problem. His sins were in the backyard of a house registered to him for many years. It is true that few people in town really knew what he looked like except to say and old man of average height with white hair and a stubbly beard on his best day.

Bobbie Kaald

Finally, with no firm decision made of what to do or not to do, the three men went to bed. In the morning, they would open the store with a small inventory and see how it went.

Finding the Family of Killers

Identifying

Michael continued his early morning to late at night obsessive shifts at James' station in the basement room. No longer clogged with dust and filth nor cluttered with furniture, it now donned fliers hanging from every vertical surface.

Michael sighed as he looked at the massive number of missing women and girls. "Now, I just have to take each photo down and list anything that might identify them." He sighed again and started. One at a time is all that he could do until they started getting calls from those people still looking for their lost one.

By the time Roberts arrived with a couple of fliers that listed items known to be with a missing girl, Michael was on his tenth

Bobbie Kaald

flier with minimal results. "About time you came to help, this is a thankless fruitless job." Seeing the fliers, he continued. "What have you got?"

"The word is slowly getting out. I have a couple of faxes from parents of missing girls in this area listing possible jewelry and purses or backpacks." Roberts stopped beside Michael to look at what he had been up to. "Does the check on the lower left corner mean that you looked at the flier?"

"Yes. One check means there wasn't anything except the picture. Two check means I have the items listed." Michael held up his yellow pad with some writing on it.

"Okay, well, let me continue with the fliers. You take these faxes and try to find the flier for the person listed. You hung them in areas? Did you label all of the area?" Roberts handed Michael the faxes as he spoke.

"I didn't originally but I moved them around with difficulty. The labels aren't overly large." Michael was realizing that the labels blended in with the large number of faxes. "I think that I will start by making bigger colored labels."

"That's a plan then." Roberts turned and looked over the fliers in front of him before going over to the desk and getting himself a yellow pad and a pen. Returning to the spot on the left of the room, he began with the next flier.

Michael came up behind him. "I just realized that I had not yet marked the flier that I just finished." He reached across

Finding the Family of Killers

Roberts and put a check on the one that Roberts was just beginning to read over. "Sorry."

"That's alright. I don't need to duplicate the work you have already done." Roberts smiled. He was glad that Michael was growing into such a meticulous individual. Turning back to the fliers, he resumed the search for items that may have survived being buried for a long period of time. This was going to take more than a week. He hoped Vincent's work would help.

It took more than a week for Vincent to feel comfortable that he had pictures of all the remains from all three sites. He had to make two trips to the one in the middle of the state. This is because the excavators were in the middle of removing the huge bushes bordering the property. It seems that they found remains poking out of the root systems for these bushes.

Roberts was opening the warehouse for the remains left to identify from before. It was their hope that someone would come forward with information that would lead to their remains being identified. Vincent was driving west now to find the bed Roberts promised him.

Vincent couldn't remember how long since he drove through the last town, but he had passed the summit more than half of an hour ago. He was tired but happy to be back with Roberts. He was thinking that after this, he might as well retire here

Bobbie Kaald

because there was enough work to keep him busy until well after that.

He saw a hand-out up ahead and pulled over for some coffee. A couple of men were off to the side looking at what seemed to be fliers. "Morning." He tried to be cordial to those around him. As he walked past, he overheard them talking about their missing daughters. Turning around, Vincent returned to them.

"Excuse me, my name is Vincent. Did I hear you say that you have daughters who are missing?" He hated speaking to the public, but he could not in good conscious let this opportunity pass.

"Yes, sir, you did. We meet here once a month to talk about them. The others will be here soon. Would you like to sit with us and wait?" The man offered because they never turned away anyone who may be in their place.

"Let me get my coffee and I will join you." Vincent decided right away that he would not show them his pictures. If it were his daughter, if he had a daughter, he would not want to see the pictures.

Vincent ordered coffee and turned to go back to the men. He braced himself and tried to turn into Roberts. He saw other men at the table now and more on the way. He stood at the edge of the table and sipped his coffee. When all the men arrived, he would tell them who he was and what he was doing here.

Finding the Family of Killers

Vincent drove away from the long coffee break. He ended up ordering food and ate it while the men made phone calls and added information to the fliers that they brought with them. He now had them on the passenger seat next to him. It was his hope this would save them some time.

Vincent drove toward Roberts home but was having trouble keeping his mind on his driving. He kept flashing back to the information he asked the men to obtain. Contact information of their address and phone number, clothing, jewelry, personal items carried, rings, watches, glasses, and anything that would stand up to being buried. He hadn't said buried, but he was certain they knew what he meant.

Eventually, Vincent stopped to get out and walk around to wake up. He entered the small store he stopped by and left with two candy bars and a large coffee. Road food, yum, but not too good for long term nutrition.

Once he was in the car with his food and drink positioned correctly, Vincent started it up for the last leg of his trip. He hoped to be there in no more than forty-five minutes at the longest. He wasn't far off. Fifty minutes later, he parked behind Roberts car.

Vincent hurried to get out because he really needed to relieve himself. Not knowing the rule for late night arrivals in a sleeping neighborhood, he slammed the door shut and ran for the house.

Bobbie Kaald

Michael opened the door for Vincent's entry. "Try not to slam the car door after ten at night. Roberts neighbors will be calling him to complain."

Vincent waved at him as he nearly ran straight into the bathroom and shut the door. He stayed in there so long that Michael became concerned, but Vincent finally appeared. "I get the couch?"

"Unless you want to sleep with me?" Michael said and laughed as he entered his own room and shut the door.

Vincent could barely stand up at this point. Mumbling under his breath, 'I'm not that desperate.' He managed to make it to the couch and sit down before his body began its sleep cycle of its own volition. He slumped slowly to the side and knew no more.

Finding the Family of Killers

Morning

After breakfast the next day, Vincent and Roberts joined James at the station. Michael had been working down below for hours already as he always did. Michael was that obsessed.

James stood up and approached the two men. "I would like to have a meeting downstairs with Michael so that we all know exactly where we stand." He didn't wait for them to respond but headed downstairs expecting them to follow.

Michael heard them coming downstairs and finished this flier before sitting down and getting ready to write notes on a fresh yellow pad. "It's about time you two got here. I know Vincent is tired, but we need to move and catch these guys."

Bobbie Kaald

"Hold your pants on. We are here now. I like the furniture arrangement. You put note pads and pens out for us, thank-you." Vincent took the desk next to Michael.

James and Roberts took the two desks across for them and waited. Roberts began by making the first remarks. "I got into the warehouse that I stored the old missing information in. Here is the disk with all of Vincent's computer-generated identities for the skulls that we found."

Vincent reached over and accepted the disk. "Thank-you. I will add this to all the photos from the three sites we are revealing. I had them box up all of the bones and possessions after I took the pictures. The boxes were sealed and numbered the same as my pictures. I have too many to count and have one disx for each site."

Michael began then, "Roberts has been helping me and we are about halfway around the room with these fliers. We are listing anything that wouldn't decompose much that may be with the remains."

Vincent interrupted. "Sorry, I forgot something. Yesterday, I stopped for coffee and found a monthly meeting of men with missing fliers. I brought the papers they gave me, and I gave them this fax number." Vincent knew it meant more work for Michael, but they were all in over their heads. "So, where do I work from?"

Finding the Family of Killers

"Washington, DC?" James jokingly asked. "We ordered a desk, and it will be here soon, but until then, you can use my desk because I will be upstairs at my real desk."

"Funny man. Thanks, sharing a desk does not bother me anymore. Laptop computers have changed my life." Vincent answered and then continued. "However, we do not have to share because I count four desks and four men."

"Okay, you have me there. I need to get back to work." James stood up and headed upstairs to leave the three men alone to get on with their work.

"Okay, I guess we should all get back to work. Michael, I will resume our work from the other side, and you can meet me in the middle. Vincent, we are listing know items on the fliers that might have survived if buried with the individual." Roberts got up and grabbed his yellow pad and pen. He knew where he left off, but he started at the beginning to verify that he had not missed a flier.

Vincent picked up his fliers and stood up. "Okay, I am going to go in order and call out the names, if either of you know where the flier is call out." This would take days and he knew that, but he needed to add his information before he started on the facial reconstructions from those already recovered.

Bobbie Kaald

Transportation

Slowly, the bones were harvested, cleaned, and packed up per Vincent's instructions. After Vincent left them, the teams in Eastern Washington began putting the boxes in all their vehicles until there was only room for the driver and a coffee cup. When the tents were empty of boxes and the equipment was loaded up, the tents came down and were pushed into the cracks over the boxes in the SUVs.

Satisfied as to the close down of the investigation area and no place to sleep, the FBI began a convoy headed to Roberts' small town. The sky was already getting dark and it was raining like no tomorrow. This drive would be long but as safe as they

Finding the Family of Killers

could make it. They found themselves wondering if there would be any place to sleep when they arrived.

The drive was slow and tedious due to week-end traffic. The lead driver didn't know the roads and nearly took the wrong turn at the bridge. Once the correct turn was accomplished, the driver nearly drove off the road when the highway turned sharply to the right. He cursed at his stupidity and rolled his window down for some fresh cool air.

The lead driver eventually became the last driver on the steep grade leading to the pass. His load must be heavier than the other vehicles. All of the drivers were very tired when they stopped along the main road through town and tried to rest some before dawn.

Their commander quietly left his vehicle and locked it. He walked across the street and knocked on the door to the police station. He waited a for a time, but no one came. The night shift must be making rounds. Sighing, he started to return to his van when he noticed a twenty-four-hour eatery. Walking down there, he hoped for coffee but when he got to the door there was a sign that they had closed early due to shortened hours.

Sighing, he walked back to his van and unlocked the door. He was tired and would rest a few hours. He hoped they would find a warehouse in lieu of his tent circus. More security and less cold at night.

In the morning, James knocked on the van's window to wake him up. It didn't take a rocket scientist to know the convoy of

Bobbie Kaald

black SUVs were driven by the FBI. "I thought you might want to go and get some breakfast." James spoke loudly when the driver stirred to continue waking him up. He would laugh if his backside weren't sticking out in the traffic.

Michael walked up beside James. "What's going on James?" He could see these were Roberts fed friends, but he didn't know why they were lined up here asleep in their SUVs.

"Not much, I'm trying to wake these guys up and go find some food for them." James answered Michael and then turned back as the window rolled down.

"Are you James? I'm looking for Roberts or Vincent." The man inside the van answered James with a question.

"Yes, I'm James. Roberts and Vincent are inside the station, I think. Michael?" James turned to Michael for confirmation.

"They left before me. I overslept and we have all eaten. I leave you to your meet and greet as they say." Michael turned and nearly forgot to look for traffic. When it was clear, he sprinted across the road and ducked into the office. He would tell the others that they were needed when he got down in the basement.

"Roberts is lining up a place. I think he wasn't expecting you so soon." James leaned up against the door to keep away from ongoing traffic.

"I need to wait here because of chain of custody." The commander started and then stopped when he saw Roberts exit

Finding the Family of Killers

the police station. "Wave him over, please. He's behind you." At the last moment, he remembered civility.

James barely turned around before Roberts stood beside him. "You two having a secret service confab outside without me?" Roberts wickedly dry sense of humor was showing brightly and then he laughed. "Vincent rented a warehouse for you. Tents are too cold and wet. Take a left at the light and make certain to slow for the railroad track or you will bottom out with your load."

"Right, is Vincent there?" The commander asked.

"He probably is, but we will be right behind you." Roberts made a note to introduce himself when they all made it to the warehouse. "James, are you coming?"

"I think Michael needs more help." James answered as he walked across the street with Roberts and then they went their separate ways.

"Roberts, I would like you to go first. We will wait for you to bring your car. There is only room for the driver because of all the boxes." The commander wasn't smiling as he called after Roberts. He needed to hurry and get out of the vehicle before he wet himself.

Bobbie Kaald

Tory

Tory and Phillip made themselves at home in the small moss encrusted rotting black mold storage of a house. Keeping Phillip fed and happy was a full-time job for Tory. He was used to it and used it as an excuse to travel. It turns out that Eastern Washington had too few sweet young things to tempt Tory.

Tory decided to take Phillip sight-seeing every weekend. Today Tory was traveling to Ross Dam with Phillip in the back seat. Phillip dropped off to sleep about an hour after they left home. This was because of the sedative Tory put in his morning juice.

Finding the Family of Killers

Tory was nearly to the beginning of the winding slowly elevating road to the top of the pass when he saw a girl hitch hiking on the side of the roadway. 'Now or never', he thought to himself. He slowed to a stop next to her and rolled down the window. "Where are you headed?" No matter where, Tory would tell her yes.

"I could use a ride. I only live two miles up the road." The pretty young blonde with a beautiful smile got inside with her packages and closed the door. She wore a white overstuffed coat and snow boots. "I think I bought too much in town. I forgot that I would have to carry it all for miles. Every mile the bags got heavier and heavier."

"Glad to be of assistance." Tory knew of an abandoned house just up the way, and he headed to that. Phillip would sleep for hours, yet. He listened to the girl chatter as he drove. Soon, he slowed down and turned right.

The blonde sat up now aware of her mistake. "You turned to soon. We were almost to my house." She began jumping around and looking back before her fear overcame her and she sat frozen in place trying to think of a way out of this.

They were in the trees by now and Tory stopped the car. "I just wanted to show you something. If you live here, you need to know about this place. I used to come here years ago. He got out and started walking around the car.

As Tory neared the passenger door, he heard the lock click into place. He didn't want to open the passenger door, but he

Bobbie Kaald

might have to. Putting his hands on his hips, he smiled the most charming smile that he could and then motioned for her to follow him. She didn't get out. He had the keys in his pocket but waited. Finally, the blonde opened the door and got out.

"I know most of this area. My friends and I came here many times." She smiled and looked at Tory who was as old as her grandfather.

"Oh, well, I haven't been here for a long time. Thank-you for humoring me." Tory smiled back at her and began to slowly walk away from the car. She kept pace with him.

Phillip woke up and looked around. It was probably the door shutting that woke him. He didn't know why he slept so long but he was feeling weak and a little dizzy when he woke up. He could see Tory and a girl up ahead in the woods and that confused him. He really needed to pee and that is probably why he woke up. It wouldn't hurt to just go to the bathroom.

Phillip watched Tory up ahead. Was that a girl next to him? He knew what Tory did to girls, like his mom. He watched Tory and quietly opened the door. Tory didn't turn around and this made Phillip happy. He got out and stood next to the car. He had to take his eyes off of Tory while he peed but when he was done, he looked again.

Finding the Family of Killers

Just as Phillip looked, the girl screamed once and was silent. Tory let her body drop where he stood. He turned to walk back and get a shovel but saw a door open.

It took only a second for Phillip to decide. He had finished and now he needed to run and save himself. It was still light out and Phillip could see where he was going but needed to hide where Tory wouldn't expect him to be.

Phillip walked quickly and quietly but didn't run because that would risk making too much noise. He really didn't know about undergrowth but there were spaces between the plants and Phillip slipped through these. The plants scratched him as he passed but he couldn't worry about that. He was going too slow, but he didn't see anywhere to hide. Tory called to him, but he ignored him and kept walking.

Phillip was taller than the plants around him but up ahead he saw a large plant growing out of a log. He looked back but didn't see Tory coming. Phillip hoped he was still busy with the girl.

When Phillip reached the plant, he crawled inside and pulled the plant back around him. He needed to sit and wait for dark to come or Tory to drive away. He was used to hiding and being quiet from when he used to hide from his mother. Tory helped him with his mother, and he was grateful, but he was afraid of Tory and his friends just the same.

Phillip was getting cold and his legs were cramping. He needed to move when he heard Tory start his car and back out onto the highway. Phillip stayed where he was for a while to

Bobbie Kaald

see if Tory parked on the road or drove away. He seemed to drive away, and still Phillip waited. After a few minutes, Phillip stretched but remained hidden. He would walk through the woods when darkness came. He would not walk toward town, and he would have to stay hidden.

Finding the Family of Killers

Vincent

Vincent picked out a spot in the corner of the warehouse and pulled a crate over to sit on. A large crate in front of him served as his table. He would make good use of his time waiting for the other agents to arrive with the remains.

When his laptop cycled up, Vincent went to work making facial reconstructions to compare with the flier photos. He planned to print them out for Michael. It would save time because he would be spending many hours, days, months with the facial reconstruction of the hundreds of skulls they found among the three properties.

Vincent unconsciously used his relaxation techniques to keep the frustration level down to a manageable level and to prevent

Bobbie Kaald

his blood pressure from skyrocketing into a stoke. This is the first case with this large number of victims. He nearly finished the first reconstruction when the convoy of black vehicles pulled in front of their new home. Vincent hoped they brought the dental specialist with them. He asked Roberts a couple of days ago to have a dental specialist brought in. Maybe James could get the local dentist to give them a couple of hours here and there.

Roberts was the first to arrive because the others needed someone to lead who had been here before. The vehicles stopped in the center of the parking area and the drivers exited at a run as their need to relieve themselves overcame their desire to maintain the chain of custody. Roberts chose to remain outside and watched the vehicles knowing exactly what they were thinking.

When the drivers returned, Roberts motioned for them to stand by before off-loading. Finally, Roberts gave a quick brief. "Vincent had the boxes numbered with a letter at the beginning. The ones starting with N and then numbers, stack on the far wall. Please try to put them in some kind of order. The ones starting with a NE will go on the wall to the right. The ones starting with a SW will go on the front wall. Alright, let's get started unloading."

Finding the Family of Killers

It took more than two hours even with Vincent's help. They ended up just putting the boxes in the general area assigned to them. Roberts was given a list of boxes for each area with their numbers. He gave this list to Vincent. "I will have Michael come down and get the boxes in order. You said that the printout of the facial identification will be printed and given to Michael?"

"That is my plan, but I don't have the printer plugged in yet." Vincent was so obsessed with the facial reconstructions that he forgot about the printer. "Did you find a dentist to help with the records? I didn't ask for dental records yet."

"No, I'm sorry. I will get with James. Okay, I am going back to talk to Michael." Roberts walked out to his car and noticed the other vehicles were now parked off to the side. As he drove away, he wondered again what they could do to find these mad murderers.

Bobbie Kaald

Tory

After Phillip disappeared into the woods, Tory buried the girl and all of her things as he usually did. He no longer buried them together as Lane and Zeke and apparently Isaac did. Bill taught him there was less chance of discovery if the evidence was simply buried wherever the event occurred.

He looked for Phillip until the sun went down and then drove away to his old stomping grounds. Caution as always was the name of the game. When he arrived, it would be after the bars closed and everyone was home sleeping. He would keep his eyes out for the local constable before leaving the road and traveling into the security of the undergrowth.

Finding the Family of Killers

Tory nearly fell asleep a couple of times before he arrived at the former mental institution. He drove through town once and saw the cruiser parked in front of the station. Smiling, Tory drove back out of town and turned onto Fruitdale Dr. A few yards down the road, Tory took a right into an overgrown lot and forced his way through.

When he was nearly at the end of the undergrowth, Tory stopped and turned off the car. Pushing his way out of the car, he held onto the door and let it close softly behind him. He didn't lock it because he might need a speedy escape.

Keeping the car to his back, Tory walked the rest of the way toward the old mental hospital. At the edge of the clearing, he stopped and looked around. What he saw was unexpected. They were constructing on the back of the building. He didn't think that would complicate him staying here as well, but it might.

It was a moonless night with no shadows. Tory took a chance and walked directly to the front door. He listened for any noise and heard only his own passing. Hidden in the entry way, Tory stood still and listened for a couple of minutes. Satisfied that he was alone, he turned and pulled out his skeleton key. If they changed the locks, this wouldn't work. Inserting the key, he turned it and opened the door.

Bobbie Kaald

Once inside, Tory locked the door again. When his eyes adjusted to the darkness, he saw that there had been some cleaning done but dust had begun to settle in again. Satisfied there was no one in this building, Tory began walking his usual route up to the room he modified for Michael and his safe room.

It took about thirty minutes for Tory to arrive using his quiet mode. When he got to his special door, it was locked from the outside. Like with club locks for cars, it could be removed but then anyone walking by could see that it was off. Tory observed this lock and looked it over from up close and far away. Finally, he decided to remove only the bolts on the right and left of the doorframe. There was a center bolt that could be loosened enough to allow Tory access and then pivot it back into place.

Tory hadn't brought any tools and had to improvise. He slowly walked around to look for anything that he could use to loosen the bolts. This quest took most of the daylight left for Tory to see with, but he did find something that could assist him. He didn't know what it was and didn't care. If it could help him, he picked it up and put it in his pocket as he continued the quest for tools.

Finding nothing else, Tory returned to his locked door. He took out his tool and began to work at the two chosen bolts. He worked slowly and laboriously trying to loosen the bolts enough to be removed with his fingers. By the time the light faded away, one of the bolts was loose enough but Tory's knuckles

Finding the Family of Killers

were bleeding. Never-the-less, Tory began work on the second bolt. This bolt loosened so quickly that Tory wished he started with this one.

Putting his tool back into his pocket, Tory removed the bolts enough to swing the bar far enough to clear the door frame. The door began to move out into the corridor just as Tory designed it to many years ago. He entered the room revealed by the door's opening and pulled it closed behind himself.

Tory sat down and leaned up against a wall. It was now too dark to see anything, but it helped him fall asleep in the comfort of a room he felt at home inside of.

When the sunlight began to filter in, Tory was already awake. He slid over to the window to monitor the outside world and see if this place became overrun with people or not. Michael and he used to sit here for three to five days without food or drink. By the time the sun went down, Tory's body needed water. He was obviously softened by his new life and knew that it was time to go.

Tory stood up in the fading light and opened the door slowly. He slid out under the bar and slipped out into the quiet of the ghostly corridor. Lining up the bar, Tory reinserted the two bolts to a point where they remained loose enough for him to remove them with his fingers. He would probably not return, but he might just buy food and fluids before returning here for another day or two.

Bobbie Kaald

Walking silently, Tory followed his own footprints in the dust out of the building. Stopping at the door to look around, he unlocked it and slid out. Turning to lock the door again, Tory ran across the open area and into the brush.

Tory forced himself to walk slowly and when he reached where his car should be, he stopped because his car was gone. "Great, I guess I will be walking, once again." He inadvertently spoke aloud and looked around to see if anyone was close by. He didn't see anyone and that was good.

Tory followed the tire tracks and headed for the road. He remembered a gas station off back the way he had come. He wouldn't get a car there, but food and water would really help right now.

Finding the Family of Killers

The Dump Sites

The collection of remains from the southern site down in the residue of volcanic ash was going slowly. The investigators used ground penetrating radar and knew there to be remains all over the field. The bad news, as there was always bad news, seemed to be that the ash was now hardened by the rain into a hard surface difficult to break.

Once they cracked the surface, it might crack into sections and it might just make a hole. Someone brought in a mace from the local hardware store, but it was back breaking work and it caused damage to the remains if they were too close to the surface.

Bobbie Kaald

Michael took a trip down there once a week to bring the boxes back with him for Vincent. The field was labeled as a grid and the boxes were labeled as to where they were found. He asked the first time only, if the personal effects were in the same box. The officer ripped his head off with offensive ear crushing terms that Michael had not heard for years. He had to stop for some Tylenol on the way home because the yelling gave him a severe headache.

Today, Michael brought down Roberts SUV because it held more, and they nearly filled it with boxes. Michael signed for the boxes and headed home.

Michael wasn't looking forward to the warehouse with its piles of boxes along the walls. This load would put the pile for the southern field higher than any others. If he knew how to help Vincent, he would because his need to identify the missing was growing every day.

When Michael entered the parking lot of the warehouse, he pulled up close to the door and parked the SUV. Michael exited quickly and walked over to the side door of the warehouse and entered. "I brought the boxes. Can anyone help unload?" He spoke loudly but continued to walk over and open the larger warehouse door.

Outside again, Michael opened all the doors to give access to the boxes. He started unloading the last to be loaded first

Finding the Family of Killers

because they went on the bottom. He really didn't expect any help on this end but was surprised by Vincent arriving to help.

"I need a break anyway. Where do we start?" Vincent asked as he saw Michael opened all the doors and already had a selected box in his arms.

"Passenger door was the last to be loaded and then the rear door." Michael nodded to the next box in the passenger seat. "I have a list of the contents in the driver's seat to give us an idea of personal belongings."

"When we finish unloading, I suggest a lunch break and then we can work together to find the flier for the facial reconstructs that I have completed." Vincent liked working with Michael because he was all work like he was. This mirrored to him the need for breaks that all of his supervisors hounded him about.

Bobbie Kaald

Sargent Salmi

Sargent Salmi just opened the door to start his shift when the phone began to ring without end. He was used to this because it happened many mornings over the years until he was forced to realize that someone watched for his arrival and spread the word.

After he took his coat off and hung it on the back of his chair and sat down at his desk, Salmi picked up the phone. "Salmi here."

"I just saw that man you were looking for last year. He stopped for gas and when he left the station, I realized that it was Quinten's car he was driving. He just left and will be driving

Finding the Family of Killers

through town any second." With that the phone made a loud click as the caller hung up hurriedly.

Salmi hung up, grabbed his coat, and was on his way to his car. He didn't take the time to lock the door in his haste. Four steps to his car door and a car drove past that he recognized as the metallic blue sedan in question. An older man was driving it, not the owner of the car.

Salmi tried to watch where the car went as he started his own, but by the time he backed out he could no longer see the car. He drove through town following the signs a visitor would take. After a turn or two, Salmi saw the blue sedan up ahead. He slowed down and followed it with three or four cars in between.

Reaching for his radio microphone, Salmi activated the push button. "Connect me to Officer James Johnson. You have the number from our investigation last year. I'll wait." He set the microphone down and monitored the car ahead of him more closely. It seemed the car was taking the back roads.

"James here? Is this Salmi?" James asked this but he knew it to be true because he was the only person who had ever contacted him via the radio before.

"Yes, but listen, Tory was spotted up here. I am following him. Head down the highway toward you, bring help. Contact me on the radio and I will let you know if he changes course. Out." Salmi gave his information and lay the microphone down. He didn't get a response and didn't expect one.

Bobbie Kaald

James hung up the phone and sprinted to the basement stairs. Pulling the door open, he yelled down the stairs. "Tory's been spotted, meet me in the cruiser." Turning around, James ran for the door and shoved it open. The door crashed open loudly and swung back again barely missing both Michael who was following him, and James who exited so loudly.

Michael climbed in the back as soon as James unlocked the cruiser. Roberts was only two steps behind and barely shut the door before James was backing out.

"Buckle up boys, this is a pursuit mode today." James turned on both lights and sirens as he shifted into drive. "We are going north, Salmi is following. Roberts contact Salmi on the radio, he's waiting to hear from us. Ask what kind of car we are looking for."

"Bossy today, aren't you James." Roberts laughed as he grabbed the microphone. "This is James Johnson's car, connect me to Sergeant Salmi, please." Roberts liked to remain polite and always had. It was even more the truth since he retired. "I will wait." Roberts braced himself as James took a turn too quickly. The siren was deafening but needed.

"Salmi here, over." The line clicked off for a response.

"James is driving. What kind of car are we looking for? Over."

Finding the Family of Killers

"Four door older blue sedan. I don't have the plates yet, but the registered owner is not driving it. Over."

"Dark blue? Over."

"Medium oxidized metallic blue. When you approach the village, turn off your lights and siren. Out." Salmi could hear the siren and understood the need but wanted to remind them to use stealth mode when they got closer.

"Out." Roberts put the microphone down and saw that they were already north of town.

"A really old blue car. Sounds like a Chevie." James was nearly to the village now and he turned off the lights and siren and slowed to the speed limit. "I hope he doesn't turn off or turns in front of us. One less killer on the road would be more than a little nice."

"Amen to that." Michael put in his two cents and moved over to the driver's side of the back seat. He wanted to be the one to find this car. He also wanted Tory arrested, not dead. He felt Tory would have Phillip with him, but he crossed his fingers just in case.

Bobbie Kaald

Phillip

Phillip waited until well after dark. His fear overwhelmed him now that he was free of the men. Also, he had fallen asleep while he waited for a time without sounds to be certain that Tory wasn't out there somewhere waiting for him to show up.

Phillip was so cold when he woke up that he could barely move. Once he did manage to stand up, he began to shiver and shake in such a way as to make it difficult to take a step. He moved slowly because of the shivers and tears formed in his eyes from the wind blowing through the trees.

Phillip began trying to walk further into the woods but made no headway and eventually risked turning around and going

Finding the Family of Killers

back to where the car of Tory's had been parked. The buses were wet from the light rain and his clothes were now dripping water. His fear built so that the shivering stopped, and he had to force himself to step out of the woods into the trail left by the car.

Phillip felt faint but relieved when he saw the car was indeed gone. He didn't want to be alone out here either and turned left to begin making his way out to the road. The wind picked up and was blowing ice pellets at him and against his bare skin. They froze against his wet clothing and turned to ice cycles and his shirt cracked and began to fall off.

Picking up the pace, Phillip nearly ran down the trail toward the road and was suddenly there. It was still dark, but a truck drove past and the gust of wind from its passing threw icy dirt crystals at him. The shivering came back and with it his teeth began to chatter so hard his jaw hurt. By now everything hurt and not realizing it, he was nearly frozen through.

The trucker must have seen him because he stopped a half mile down the road and got out. Phillip needed help but began to walk the other way, backward. Seeing this, the trucker called out. "Let me help you, the cab is nice and warm. I will take you to town and find some help if you need it." The trucker stopped walking toward the boy and wondered if his voice carried that far.

Phillip stopped and looked at the man. He could hear him saying something, but the words were unintelligible at this

Bobbie Kaald

distance. He knew that he needed help, and this wasn't Tory. Making up his mind to risk it, Phillip began walking toward the trucker. His slow progress caused the trucker to walk up to Phillip and lift him up.

The trucker carried him back to his cab and with great difficulty, and some assistance from Phillip, they climbed into the cab. "Crawl into the back and cover up while I drive. If you don't get pneumonia from this, you will be a lucky boy." With that said, the trucker resumed driving. His engine remained on the entire rescue operation and he pulled away from the curb as quickly as an eighteen-wheeler can.

Finding the Family of Killers

The Call

Later that same morning, James was preparing to leave his office for a meeting with the mayor. The phone rang and James chose to ignore it but after so many rings that his head hurt, he answered it. "Hello?"

"I have a call for you from Central Washington State Patrol office. Hold please." A woman's voice spoke in a nearly robotic fashion and James almost hung up. He would be late.

"Officer Johnson?" A man's voice came on.

"Yes?" James was too impatient with the caller and he knew it but couldn't bring out his polite self.

"A trucker brought a young boy in this morning suffering from exposure. He likely has pneumonia. The only thing that

Bobbie Kaald

anyone got out of him is a man named Tory kidnapped him and he just got away. The trucker found him on the highway outside of Winthrop." The man paused to let this sink in.

"We thought we had Tory cornered but he got away. His car was found abandoned in a shopping area. He stole another car and is being hunted." James stopped talking because he wasn't addressing the Trouper's immediate concerns. "Which hospital did you say?" He got the name and hung up. He left his office and went to see Michael.

Opening the door, James called for Michael. "Michael pack and overnight bag and find Roberts. When I get back, we head for Eastern Washington." He didn't wait for an answer but should have because Michael wasn't down there. The Mayor needed to be placated and that is all James was really thinking about.

When James returned, Michael was no where around. James descended into the basement and found it empty. Sighing, he climbed back up to get into his car for a drive around to see if they went to the warehouse.

At the last second, James took some deep breaths and got a grip on his impatience. Stopping in his tracks, he returned to his office and began making phone calls. His first call was to the warehouse without success. His second phone call was to

Finding the Family of Killers

Roberts and Michael's shared home to no avail. Stumped, James walked out to his cruiser and used his radio to try to find Roberts.

After leaving a message for them to find Roberts, James started the engine and drove off to fill up at the city gas pump. He left the door open while he filled the tank and was just about to get back inside of his cruiser when the radio called his name. "Officer Johnson here, out."

"I have Roberts. One moment." The woman clicked off and Roberts was there.

"What is it James?" Roberts sounded extremely tired.

"A State Trouper called. I believe that the kidnapped boy has been found. A boy was brought in by a trucker with exposure. I was going to drive over and see the boy. Where are you? Over." James wanted to leave and was impatient to get on the road.

"Michael is with me. We are trying to find Tory. You go and call me when you know anything. Out." Roberts wanted to go but he needed to find Tory if he was still on this side of the mountains and Michael look distressed at having to choose where to go.

James shrugged his shoulders and closed the door. He could go on his own. He preferred for Roberts to come or Michael, but they needed to do so much with so few people that this was the best decision.

Bobbie Kaald

James drove up to the hospital about two in the afternoon. He pushed his speed some by turning on his light as he drove empty roads through the canyon. When he was approaching cities though, James drove without excess speed and turned his light off for caution.

The slow drive allowed him time to center and calm down somewhat. He avoided stopping for coffee because he needed to be calm when he approached the boy. James hoped the boy remembered his name and where he came from because he didn't bring any fliers with him. He should have looked for the one mentioning the boy.

Finding the Family of Killers

The Capture

Roberts and Michael drove the back roads from south to north. They already went from the Village where Tory stole his last car down to the police station and were now driving the back roads from town to the lake and around.

Roberts turned right after a gas station grocery store and over a bridge. It was dark now and he was just driving. Michael was trying to look both ways with a new toy they obtained from the FBI office. Michael could see like a cat in the dark with these special binoculars.

"Let's start on the left this time. Watch for bushes broken apart by a car driving through." Michael spoke for the first time in the last hour.

Bobbie Kaald

"Any turn is as good as any other. I haven't heard from James yet. I hope the boy was the kidnapped victim. That will be a great weight off my mind." Roberts answered as he made a left. He didn't care if they were dead end roadways or not, he wanted to cover all the roads. If the house was lived in with many cars out front, he mentally crossed them off of his mind.

"That's all that I can think about." Michael admitted but did not take his eyes off of his search. "We waste too much time going everywhere together. This is more productive."

"I agree with you. We need everyone to look for these men and I hope James brings the boy back to his family. Working together only helps some. Vincent is making facial identification picture and decided to scan the fliers into his computer. We can do more by spending time searching for where he holed up at." Roberts stopped talking as the reached the end of the road.

"Drive out and we can look some more on the way out." Michael hadn't seen anything but wanted to try again.

It was nearing dawn without success and Roberts pulled over to the side for a quick break. There was a property without a house on it filled with trees and long grass. The two men quietly opened their doors and quickly relieved themselves.

Finding the Family of Killers

As they closed their doors, a car entered the road behind them. Roberts let it drive by and he just couldn't believe it. Tory sat behind the wheel as plain as day. "Michael, get down."

Michael dropped down out of conditioning and Roberts started his car but left the lights off. Pulling out, he began to tail his prey. He would not lose Tory tonight. "Michael, get on the radio and let the State Troopers and County Sheriff's know what is going on. By the time they get everyone to report in, we should have a position."

Roberts followed as close as he could and eventually, Tory turned off. Roberts parked his car and he left Michael in the car to contact everyone.

Roberts ran along the edge of the road and nearly broke his leg once. He succeeded in finding where Tory went off the road and followed until he saw the car. Turning around, Roberts went back to his own car.

"Did he stop for the night?" Michael asked the big question.

"Looks like it." Roberts asked as he called in their position. "Now, we wait."

Twenty minutes later, the road was lined with vehicles. The signal to go was given and the men began entering the woods and surrounded the car. When they reached the car, the man was asleep.

Bobbie Kaald

Roberts knocked on the window and when the man sat up, he opened the door. "Tory, it's over." He would have been more than a little upset if it were not Tory, but Michael came up after Tory was secured and identified him.

When the FBI had Tory secured, the sheriff's towed the car and would return it to the owner after it was processed. Roberts and Michael headed home and to bed. In the morning, they would try to reach James to see about the boy.

Finding the Family of Killers

The Boy

James found the boy at the hospital alright. The boy was unconscious and had been from the minute he crawled into the back of the cab. He was carefully lifted out of the truck with a great deal of difficulty. There were cuts and abrasions but no broken bones. Testing found no sign of a concussion and only a slight amount of fluid in the lungs which cleared once he was warm enough.

James sat at his beside wishing that Michael were here to talk to him and help him come to grips with his fears. Eventually, James walked out to the nurse's station and left his information for the local motel. He just needed to eat and sleep. When he woke up, he hoped the boy would be awake.

Bobbie Kaald

On his way to the restaurant, James radio went off as usual, but this time it was his name. Picking up the microphone, "Officer Johnson here, out."

"This is Michael, out." Michael's voice came out of the speaker.

"Good, I've seen the boy but his hasn't woken up. Are you two at a place where you can at least fax the flier for the boy who we think he is to the local station? Out." James kept driving and was nearly there. His stomach rumbled loudly from neglect.

"We found Tory. He is with the FBI and facing many charges. Roberts and I are on the way over with the flier. Out." Michael looked at Roberts who was driving for confirmation.

Roberts nodded and just kept driving with his eyes on the road. This was the hardest part of the drive through the canyon.

"I'm grabbing some food and have a room at our usual motel. See you when you get here. Out." James pulled into the restaurant and parked his car. Maybe he should just go to the motel. He sighed and got out to stick to his original plan.

Roberts found James in his motel room, but James was too asleep and could not be aroused. Roberts motioned for Michael to leave and followed him outside. "We can go alone up to the hospital. Maybe you can talk to the boy about your experience

Finding the Family of Killers

when you were first captured. Try not to talk about anything overly awful."

Michael didn't say anything for a while but got back into the car wishing he had done more stretching. "The flier says that he is about eleven, brown hair, and blue eyes. We don't have a height, but his name is Scott."

"I'm glad you remembered to bring that flier." Roberts was approaching the hospital and used caution with driving because of the increased traffic.

"I didn't remember. This is a copy that I put in my pocket long ago, just in case." Michael knew he was too close to the case, but he wasn't a hardened career officer. He now knew that the hardness was just a cover in most cases.

"Should I be worried?" Roberts asked as he pulled into his parking spot. He looked directly in Michael's eyes and waited for an answer.

"No, because I am aware that I am too emotionally involved in this case, but I needed for the boy to be removed from the influence of these killers." Michael said and got out of the car. Closing the door behind him, he leaned against the car and forced himself to relax at least a little. Still tense, Michael stood away from the car and followed his friend into the hospital.

Roberts stopped at the front desk and asked where the John Doe young boy was. The operator gave him a room number and pointed in the right direction. "Thank you for your help."

Bobbie Kaald

Roberts and Michael walked around and eventually found the room guarded by local officers. "Hi, James is sound asleep, and this is Michael, and I am Roberts, I was with the FBI."

"Good timing, he just woke up. The nurse is with him now. She will call the doctor if there is a need." The officer did not get up and returned to reading the newspaper.

Roberts and Michael looked at each other and both of them raised their eyebrows but said nothing. They leaned up against the wall and waited. A couple of minutes later the nurse came out. "Do they check out?" The older mother type nurse asked the local officer.

"We been expecting them." The officer answered her while still reading his newspaper.

The nurse turned back to Roberts and Michael. "Can I see your IDs?"

"Certainly." Roberts pulled out his driver's license and his retirement card. Michael had a deputy card but no license.

"Okay, but there was another officer here earlier." She looked at their IDs and moved away from the door.

Roberts and Michael entered the room slowly because they didn't want to frighten the boy any more than he already was. He was awake and looking at them.

"Hi. My name is Michael, and we are going to try to get you back home." Michael thought this would be a good place to start. He was concerned with the blonde hair at first. As he got

Finding the Family of Killers

closer to the bed, he could see brown roots showing and this gave him some relief.

"I don't have a home. Tory killed my mom." Phillip as he now thought of himself answered and rolled over.

"You don't know me, but I was taken by these men long ago just as you have been. They killed my mom as well, but Roberts and James helped me find other family. I brought a flier for a missing boy for you to look at. You can tell me if this is you or not." Michael pulled out the flier and began to unfold it.

This must have interested the boy because he rolled back over to look at what Michael was doing because he could hear paper rattling. "What is that?"

"It has a picture of a missing boy on it. It says he has brown hair but yours is blonde." Michael began a verbal game with the boy to help him relax and take charge if he would.

"I let them bleach my hair. I always wanted to, but my mom wouldn't let me." The boy was smiling now and seemed to be more relaxed than before.

"Why don't you look at this and tell me what you think?" Michael held out his paper flier to the boy because in his heart he knew this was a living boy from the missing flier.

The boy took the paper and looked it over slowly before giving it back to Michael. "It looks like me, but it can't be because it says I have a grandmother and I don't think I have one. At least ways, I don't have a living grandmother."

Bobbie Kaald

"We will need to test your DNA and her DNA to be certain, but it might be possible. That happened to me." Michael spoke slowly and tried to think of the best way to explain it to the boy. "I would like to call you by the name on the flier then if that is okay with you."

"Tory had me pick a name, Phillip is the one that I chose. Scott was my name before as the flier says." With that Phillip became Scott, and felt a great burden lift off of him and the tears started to flow for a long time.

Michael let him cry because it was good for him and walked back over to where Roberts was standing and quietly listening. "I think he is the Scott that the flier is talking about."

"I believe you are correct. Can you ask him if they visited any of Tory's friends?" Roberts spoke softly but Scott heard him and answered.

"Yes, we stayed with Isaac and Zeke and Lane at three places just for a short time each place." Scott was laying on his back in the bed watching them. His face was still wet, but his tears had stopped. "How long do I have to stay here?"

"Until the Doctor releases you. What were these places?" Michael didn't ask where but what because Scott would know that the best.

"Let me think. Right after Tory took me out of my home, I think we went to a junkyard. From there we stayed in a different place every night for a while. Eventually, we ended up

Finding the Family of Killers

eating at a restaurant where we found Isaac. We left with him and Zeke stayed with Lane at the bakery across the street. It must not have worked out because they showed up at Isaac's new place a couple of weeks later. Tory and I left a few days after that. Did that help much?" Phillip sat up then and started smiling because it felt good to help these two men who seemed to be friends.

"It does. I think I forgot to tell you that Tory has been arrested and will be charged with your kidnapping and your mother's murder among other things." Michael told him and then asked Roberts something under his breath. "We are going to buy you some new clothes to wear when the doctor says that you may leave."

Roberts saw Scott getting upset. "We won't be long. Don't be upset."

"Okay, cowboy clothes?" Scott had wanted cowboy clothes as long as he could remember. "Size twelve." He called after them and hoped they heard.

Bobbie Kaald

The Article

The media didn't take long before they published an article about Scott. They didn't care that the boy barely knew his own name or that his mother was murdered. It was news and they printed up as much as they knew and what they suspected.

Roberts was furious as was James. They were able to get the doctor to release the boy and took him home with them right away. Soffia was more than happy to watch out for Scott until his grandparents arrived. The DNA tests were sent and were pending but everyone felt certain Scott and the mother's parents would be together soon.

Finding the Family of Killers

At breakfast, Isaac and Lane and Zeke were sharing the paper as per usual when Zeke saw the article. "We can eat later. He put a twenty on the table and got up to leave."

Without question, his two friends left without so much as another sip of coffee. They did take the paper with them.

Lane was the first one to reach the car and climbed into the driver's side. He started the car as the other two climbed in. As Lane backed out and began driving out of town, Isaac took the paper that Zeke was holding and glanced over it. Scanning the lead article, he put the paper down after an expletive of a creative nature.

"Okay, why are we leaving?" Lane asked the air because for some reason these two weren't talking.

"A boy was rescued and taken to the hospital. He spoke with Agent Roberts." Zeke managed to spit out and cursed. "Tory has been arrested for kidnapping and they are looking for the three of us."

"They have our names?" Lane asked.

"Unknown, but that boy is a smart kid." Isaac answered and then the car went silent as they headed out of this small town where everyone knew their faces and names. Isaac was once again losing his business and the start-up money. He wasn't happy.

Zeke asked to be let out at the first large parking lot they came to. "It's been nice, but time to split up the group. Every

Bobbie Kaald

man for himself. Stay safe." He got out and began looking for a likely car to steal as he walked toward the store.

Isaac looked at Lane and nodded. They drove further through the parking lot and parked the now tainted car. Both got out and looked for a new car. Isaac wanted to take his camping gear with him but opted to buy new as per his usual way of doing things. He would need to stop by his own personal stash and pick up some living money.

The three men each left the parking lot in a newly stolen car. They needed to time this right or the police would be called and one of them would be trapped in the act. The idea was to drive in different directions and disappear into the countryside. They were accustomed to this and did it well. They all knew the rules learned long ago and followed them scrupulously.

All things considered the three men had a good run and lived free the entire time. None of the three men wanted to join Tory in the cell or in a different cell. So, they drove away to preserve their freedom and find new homes and identities.

Finding the Family of Killers

Cold Case Again

Scott road back across the pass with Michael and Roberts. He was on cloud nine. Michael brought him cowboy clothes at his request, but he bought all the trimmings, too. Scott was the proud owner of a white cowboy hat, a toy gun and holster set, and boots with spurs and lots of silver that sparkled when he walked.

"Looks like I'm a big hit with the boy." Michael was in the front with Roberts and the boy was in the back. James left earlier with the boy's DNA collection. He was to deliver it to the FBI office closest to home. He also had a copy of the boy's missing person flier.

Bobbie Kaald

"It was worth the money to see his sad eyes light up." Roberts was extremely happy to be party to finding a victim still alive and to do something over the edge nice for him. "The FBI has the DNA from the crime scene to compare it to what James will provide to them. It should match and the grandparents will be notified at that point. No one wants to get their hopes up until we know for certain."

"They don't live too far away." Michael hadn't contacted his extended family for a long time but planned to after this. "I am thinking it is a good thing they lived close to their daughter."

"James called Soffia and she has permission to be his caregiver until the grandparents arrive. It turns out she got a foster parents license after Helena and just never used it. Scott will be in good hands with her." Roberts and Michael had talked to Scott about this and James was with Scott when they returned with his present of the cowboy outfit. The doctor discharged him into their care and James signed for Scott.

James should have done the transport, but Scott wanted to go with Michael. No one wanted to traumatize the boy any further. And so, Roberts drove to James house and left Scott with Soffia for now. When they left Soffia was showing Scott to a bed and gave him one of James undershirts to sleep in. The last that they heard was Scott asking for pancakes for breakfast.

Finding the Family of Killers

Vincent managed to identify several of the victims in each site. Most had no family left looking for him. A few families came to claim the remains and thank them for letting them know what happened to their little girl. They were all little girls at two of the sites and a mixture where the plant roots needed to be removed from the skeletal remains.

When Vincent had done his best, the boxes were labeled and place back in the warehouse. Michael kept his fliers up for a long time. Eventually, the basement was locked to preserve the investigation area if the case ever heated up again.

The police continued to watch for the men without success. Isaac's two businesses were both investigated and fingerprints were everywhere. Scott's fingerprints were not in the bakery. None of the fingerprints were in the system and this seemed very unlikely.

Scott's grandparents were located and came to talk to James as he was the lucky one to call them and relay that their grandson was alive. "I am glad to finally meet you. My wife is bringing Scott over and that will give us time to talk." James greeted them and sat with them on the lobby couches. "Help yourself to coffee if you like."

"We are fine. Is Scott okay?" The grandmother asked. "We have been so worried. I was relieved when you called. Is it really Scott?" She spoke fast and played with her hands in a nervous fashion.

Bobbie Kaald

"The DNA confirms he is Scott. The doctor cleared him to come back with us. They said he had exposure and was simply tired and not in a coma as they originally thought." James sat with them and slowly went over Scott's condition. "Scott did give us some names and we would like you to bring him in for visits once in a while. We want another try to get him together with our newest officer who is also an artist. If Scott can help make sketches of the men, it will be a big start toward catching them."

"We will talk it over with Scott and call you back. Can I have a card with your number on it?" The grandfather turned and looked when the door opened letting in a cool breeze and that finished their conversation.

Scott was the first one in the door. He ran to James, not the strangers to him at first. "James, can I see the jail?"

"Scott, these are your mother's parents, your grandparents. They have come to take you to live with them." James eyes were tearing just a little because he was going to miss Scott.

Scott stopped just short of hugging James and turned with his backside touching James. He looked long and hard at the people across from him. "Hello. You're my grandparents? Momma said we were alone."

"Yes, we are Scott. Your mother and I had a fight, and she took you away when you were much younger. We tried to find

Finding the Family of Killers

you two, but now we only have you." His grandmother stopped talking and began to cry.

"I hope you are okay with coming home with us. You can start school when you are ready. Perhaps you might like to talk to a doctor about your experiences and how it made you feel. If so, we will arrange that." The grandfather took over but started babbling and James had to interfere.

"Scott, I think your grandfather is just nervous. There will be many new things for you and feelings that you may or may not experience in the future. Your grandparents will be there for you when you need them. No one can take the place of your mama, but they will be your family." James looked Scott right in the eye as he spoke.

"You want me to go home with them?" Scott came to his own conclusion without being told.

"Yes. I have liked you staying with me, but they can be a firm foundation for your future." James explained to him already about foster care and the temporariness of his stay with Soffia.

"A new adventure, right." Scott turned back around and held out his hand to James. They shook hands very formally. "Bye, for now." Turning back around, Scott walked over to his grandparents who were both standing now. They hugged and left the office to begin Scott's new life. They forgot the business card.

Bobbie Kaald

Finding the Family of Killers

Made in the USA
Middletown, DE
23 January 2021